THE CROWN JEWELS MYSTERY

THE CROWN JEWELS MYSTERY

AVA & CAROL DETECTIVE AGENCY

THOMAS LOCKHAVEN

TWISTED KEY
publishing

2019

First Printing: 2019

ISBN 978-1-947744-35-6

Twisted Key Publishing, LLC
www.twistedkeypublishing.com

Ordering Information:
Special discounts are available on quantity purchases by corporations, associations, educators, and others. For details, contact the publisher at the above listed address.

U.S. trade bookstores and wholesalers: Please contact Twisted Key Publishing, LLC by email twistedkeypublishing@gmail.com.

CONTENTS

1 Purple Bangs 1

2 The Contest 5

3 The Secret Clues 9

4 The First Clue 13

5 Saint Thomas's Church 18

6 I'm Falling for You.. 25

7 I See You.. 29

8 The Local News 32

9 Captain Parker 37

10 Flower Injustice 43

11 Apple Orchard 52

12 The Orchard House.. 60

13 Scream 66

14 That's a Lot of Squares 71

15 Sleepy Hollow Cemetery 78

16 The Cipher 83

17 Gallagher's Inn 87

18 The Chase.. 97

19 Forgiveness.. 107

20 Now I Get It.. 112

Author's Note.. 115

1
PURPLE BANGS

"I always want to say 'foiled again' when I get my hair colored," Ava mentioned.

"I know. You tell me *each* time you get your hair colored," replied Carol, "and it wasn't funny the first time."

"Maybe it's my delivery."

"Maybe it's just not funny," suggested Carol.

"You're not funny."

"Okay," moaned Carol, "and *down* we spiral."

"What are you two jabbering about?" asked Kaitlyn as she checked the progress of Ava's highlights.

"My comedic prowess," Ava explained.

"We were both agreeing that it doesn't exist," added Carol.

"I was telling Carol that when you foil my hair, I always wanted to say, 'Aha! Foiled again.'"

"Sorry, Aves," smiled Kaitlyn, giving Carol a wink. "Just not feeling it."

"Nothing? Maybe it's my timing?"

"Not to change the subject," said Kaitlyn, clearing her throat, "but I thought you two would be all over the contest in the paper."

"The *what*?" asked Ava, winking.

"The newspaper," Carol deadpanned. "It's the internet for old people."

"Ah," laughed Kaitlyn, pointing a brush at Carol. "Now, see? *That* was funny."

"Yeah, yeah, yeah. So, what's this contest?" asked Ava.

"Some guy named Connor Bishop—he's supposed to be some millionaire philanthropist," Kaitlyn explained, arching her finely manicured eyebrows. "Anyways, he's running a scavenger hunt of sorts, and whoever solves the clues and finds the treasure gets $10,000."

"That kind of money is gonna bring in treasure hunters from all over," mused Carol.

"One second," said Kaitlyn, retrieving a folded newspaper from a table covered with magazines and brochures. "Ignore the coffee stains," she laughed. "Give me a second." Kaitlyn flipped through the newspaper until she found the local section. "Here's the article." She jabbed at a picture of a diamond pendent with the headline, "Solve the clues, win $10,000."

"May I?" asked Carol, reaching for the paper.

"Certainly," replied Kaitlyn as she handed over the newspaper.

"How do you turn this thing on?" joked Carol, flipping the newspaper around.

"Savage," laughed Kaitlyn. "You're just too funny."

"I'm a natural," gushed Carol. "What can I say? Okay, let's get down to business." Carol snapped her wrist, bringing the newspaper to attention. She cleared her throat and read:

Do you think you have what it takes to solve the mystery behind the famous Crown Jewels of Ireland theft? Connor Bishop of Viva Renaissance, Inc., would like to offer you the unique opportunity to test your skills in this fun recreation of the original Crown Jewels, stolen in 1907 from the Dublin Castle in Ireland.

Everyone will be provided with a set of clues that must be solved to find the Crown Jewels. The first person to locate the treasure will receive a cash prize of $10,000.

Visit the website link below to register. Everyone who registers will receive an email with the clues on Wednesday, August 17 at 8 a.m. Good luck!

"That's tomorrow!" exclaimed Carol excitedly. "We've got to sign up." She slipped her bedazzled phone out of her pocket and snapped a picture of the advertisement.

"I wonder how many people are going to sign up?" asked Ava. "I mean, with a $10,000 cash prize…."

"It's gonna bring out some of the most experienced treasure hunters!" Carol cried. "Ava, it's our chance to pit our skills against the best of the best!"

"All right," said Kaitlyn, checking Ava's hair one last time. "Your highlights look amazing." She turned Ava's chair to face the mirror.

"I look stunning," gushed Ava, "but only because I have the most talented hairstylist in the world."

"It's true," laughed Kaitlyn, unfastening Ava's smock. "So," she said mischievously, brushing aside a blond flyaway, "when you two sleuths win the $10,000, I'll be expecting a finder's fee."

"You got it," smiled Carol, knowing all too well that Kaitlyn was of course kidding. But, being a single mom with a physically challenged child, she could really use the money.

She looked at the narrow shelf beneath the mirror where Kaitlyn kept all of her things. There sat a picture of her daughter London: a miniature version of Kaitlyn, tall and thin with high cheekbones and chocolate-brown eyes. London was deaf, and Kaitlyn had been saving for a cochlear implant so that her daughter could hear.

Carol knew that Ava would agree that if they won the contest, they would donate it all to little London.

2
THE CONTEST

Ava and Carol could hardly wait to get to The Lair, their secret hideout located in the basement of Ava's house. The Lair was the ultimate crime-solving laboratory. After each case, the girls would take a bit of their earnings and use the money to add new equipment.

The girls swung their bikes into the driveway, skidding to a stop behind Ava's house. The pair had their own entrance to The Lair: through a back door in the basement, which was equipped with a motion detector and a camera.

"All right," said Ava, making a beeline for her laptop. She flipped open the lid and swooshed her finger across the touchpad. "Let's get registered." She angled the laptop toward Carol so they could both see the screen.

Ava typed in the web address and pressed Enter. The page loaded, turning Ava's screen black. Suddenly, golden letters magically appeared on the screen as if drawn by an invisible paintbrush.

Viva Renaissance, Incorporated, mouthed Ava.

The words dissolved, and a man in an impeccable, gray linen suit appeared on the screen. "Greetings," the man spoke in a clipped British accent. "I am Connor Bishop, historian, philanthropist, and renaissance man."

"Modest," interjected Carol without missing a beat.

The man paused and then furrowed his brow as if about to describe an abysmal act that had just taken place. "In 1907, an egregious act of betrayal occurred when the Crown Jewels of Ireland were stolen. Vanished into thin air. There are many conspiracies as to how they were stolen." He paused dramatically. "Now, it's up to you...," he pointed at the screen, "...to help find them."

The stolen jewels appeared, spinning on the screen, sparkling and shining. The first jewel was the Grand Master's diamond star, the centerpiece of the Crown Jewels, made up of four hundred Brazilian diamonds, and at its center, a shamrock of emeralds set on a ruby cross.

"That's gorgeous," declared Ava. "So sparkly."

The Grand Master's diamond star dissolved into dust, and the next piece of jewelry appeared: the Grand Master's diamond badge. This piece of jewelry featured a diamond-encrusted crown atop an angelic golden harp of diamonds. A circular badge was attached to the bottom of the harp, surrounded by Brazilian stones, and in the center of the badge, red rubies formed an "X," with an emerald-green shamrock in the middle.

Just like its predecessor, the Grand Master's diamond badge dissolved into a cloud of golden dust.

The last image was the Collar Badge of Knight Companion. To Ava, it looked more like a fancy, oversized charm bracelet. The collar was made of harps and roses tied together with knots of gold. The petals of the roses alternated between white leaves within red and red leaves within white. In the center of the collar was an imperial jeweled crown mounted over a harp of gold.

The necklace vanished, and Connor Bishop reappeared, a huge smile on his face.

"Join me, Connor Bishop, on this exciting quest by filling out the form below. Then, watch for an official email from me, where I will include the rules of the contest and the clues. Good luck and Godspeed!"

A disclaimer appeared at the bottom of the video, informing the viewers that these were not the actual Irish Crown Jewels, but a realistic representation created by famed jeweler Hans Müller. A counter at the bottom showed how many people had entered the contest.

"Geez," whispered Ava. "Over three hundred people so far."

"That is a lot of people," agreed Carol, "but I have to assume that the clues will be extremely difficult. I mean, with a reward of $10,000, they can't make it easy."

The girls turned in unison—a soft chime had just alerted them that someone was at the door. Ava clicked the security icon on her laptop. The door camera revealed a thin young man with shaggy blond bangs hanging over his eyes.

He swished his head to the side, revealing dazzling blue eyes for an instant, only to once again have them covered by his bangs.

"It's Derik," chirped Carol, smiling. She pushed Ava's shoulder, nearly knocking her to the floor, and clicked on the speaker icon. "Hey, Derik. I'll be right there."

"Thanks," he said, waving at the camera.

Derik Charter was a close friend and classmate of the girls. A few months earlier, they had helped Derik's father when his bank had been robbed.

"Hey, Derik," said Carol, smiling and waving him inside. "What's up?"

"Hey, Carol. Hey, Ava," waved Derik.

"Hi Derik," smiled Ava, laughing at how excited Carol was to see him.

"Well, actually, my dad kind of put me up to this," he admitted somewhat tentatively. "I think it's mostly to get me out of the house, and you can say no, and it'll be totally cool—"

"Dude," interrupted Ava. "Out with it."

"Sorry," exclaimed Derik, his face turning bright red. "My dad saw some treasure contest on the news last night, and he thought that maybe the three of us could, you know, form a team."

"That would be awesome," nodded Carol. "I mean, don't you agree, Aves?"

"Wait, you guys already know about—"

"Connor Bishop, the Crown Jewels, the year 1907.... Yes, Derik. Look at us. We are professional investigators. Of course we know," declared Ava.

"I'm digging the new highlights, Ava," said Derik, turning on the charm. "Did you go to Kaitlyn?"

"He's in," declared Ava, waving her arms. "The man obviously has a refined sense of taste. Now, let's get registered."

3
THE SECRET CLUES

Derik, Ava, and Carol sat gathered around Ava's laptop. Ava's mom had brought down blueberry pancakes, scrambled eggs, bacon, and orange juice for everyone.

"Two more minutes before Connor Bishop's email goes out," whispered Carol excitedly.

Ava, Carol, and Derik had spent the previous evening brainstorming the most effective way to decipher the clues. They set up a large table and placed three laptops side by side so they could all work together. Ava suggested that they use the crime board—a giant rolling magnetized whiteboard—to display the clues.

While Derik and Ava set up the workstations, Carol researched the history behind the Crown Jewels, learning everything she could about their theft. There were many suspects, and many anonymous tips as to their whereabouts, but to this day they had not been found.

Ava let out an audible gasp. "It's here!" An email entitled *Crown Jewels Competition* appeared in the inbox. Derik and Carol stood on either side of her, leaning in to see her screen.

"Should I read it out loud?" Ava inquired.

"Sure," encouraged Carol. "Let me know if you need any help with the big words."

"Funny," muttered Ava. "If sleuthing doesn't work out for you, I'm sure you could get a gig as a clown."

"Go ahead, Ava," urged Derik, winking at Carol.

"Thank you, Derik." Ava cleared her throat and began:

Dear Competitor,

Welcome to this exciting adventure. First, a bit of important history, and then the clues. As you know, in 1907, the Crown Jewels were stolen and were never seen again. In honor of this enduring mystery, Viva Renaissance, Incorporated has created a series of clues that lead to the mock jewels, created by world-renowned jeweler Hans Müller.

"Hans **Müller** the jeweler," snorted Ava. "How perfect." She continued reading,

Lastly, we've hidden these jewels where only the most clever and brave will be able to find them. Return them to me at 157 West Main Street, and I will personally give you $10,000 in cash!

Download the clues. Good luck and Godspeed.

"All right." Ava rubbed her hands together, getting caught up in the moment. "You guys ready?" She clicked the download link and pressed Print.

Carol and Derik nodded in unison; they couldn't have been more ready.

"Fancy," declared Ava. "He made it look like it was handwritten on an old piece of paper." She held up the image for them to see.

"He wants it to be authentic-looking," suggested Carol. "Do you want me to read it?"

"No, I got this," said Ava, shaking her head. She began to read.

I am neither man, nor woman, nor beast, nor fowl. Yet, by glass and mirrors, I see beyond. Frozen, upon my perch I stand. Worship below, the ancients desired my luster, the sun forever setting at my back.

Where the road divides, stands a warrior in repose. Beneath his shadow, the living mirror lies. Written within, by neither feather nor pen. Without it, life would die.

From my orchard, I place an apple on the mantel above my fire. Hidden in the arch, you will find what you desire. An orchard of sisters, an intellect, a muse, a teller of little stories, my name but a ruse.

Ichabod's home, now a place of mortality. A circular stone, suggests punctuality. I depend on a star for the passage of time. Upon the hour of three, follow the line. The first chiseled words will reveal to you, the path that is just, the path that is true.

Ava looked up at Carol and Derik and shook her head. "And I thought interpretive poetry was difficult."

Carol nodded. Ava could tell her wheels were already spinning. "Let's get it up on the crime board, and we'll start picking apart the clues there." Carol's tone was all business.

"Derik, you've got the best handwriting," said Ava, printing a copy of the email and clues. "Will you write the clues on the crime board?"

"I'm on it," said Derik, hurrying over to the printer.

"All right," said Carol. "Fire up Google. We're going to break this thing…like…wide open," she said finally.

"Couldn't think of anything to say after 'break this thing,' could you?" Ava teased.

"Nope," blushed Carol. "And we're moving on."

4
THE FIRST CLUE

Ava, Carol, and Derik sat behind a long card table, made up of three independent stations. Each station had a laptop, a notepad, a bottle of water, and an aqua-blue Charter Bank stress ball, courtesy of Derik's dad.

"All right," began Carol, "I think we should break the first series of clues into their most basic elements and then go from there." She directed her attention to Derik. "Do you mind manning the crime board?"

"I'm on it," he exclaimed.

"Okay," she continued as Derik hustled over to the board. "The beginning starts with the phrase *I am neither man, nor woman, nor beast, nor fowl.*"

"So...not living?" offered Derik.

"I'm not sure yet," said Carol, staring at the board. "Just start a column with the key elements, and then we'll try to figure out what each one means."

"All right, then. The next clue is, *Yet, by glass and mirrors, I see beyond,*" recited Derik, writing, and then he continued, "*Frozen, upon my perch I stand.*"

"Wait a minute," ventured Ava. "I know we're going to break this down and then try to figure it out. But it says that it's neither man, nor woman, nor beast, nor fowl, so how can it stand upon a perch? And how can it see? Those are things that a living being would do."

"I know," nodded Carol. "I had the exact same thoughts. Let's just work our way through the clues, and then we'll attack."

Derik moved ahead through the clues and wrote, *Worship below*, *the ancients desired my luster*, and *sun forever setting at my back*.

"Perfect," nodded Carol. "So, we've got a column of six clues."

"Wait," said Derik excitedly. "Could it be a tree? It's a living thing. It's neither man, nor woman, nor beast, nor fowl! Its perch could be a hill or a mountain. People have always worshiped beneath trees. Many desire trees for shade, paper, wood, and— depending on where the tree is—the sun would forever be setting on its back."

"I'm not hating the idea," admitted Carol, nodding.

"I'm not either," said Ava. "Except for the fact that it ignores the second and third clues, *By glass and mirrors*, and, *I see beyond*. I'm pretty sure those clues are talking about a telescope, like the one my dad gave us. And to help solidify my point, when I Googled *seeing beyond mirror and glass*, one of the results was a refractory telescope."

"Of course!" nodded Carol. "To see beyond, you would use a telescope."

"Sorry, Derik," smiled Ava. "I didn't mean to burst your bubble."

"Hey." Derik threw up his hands. "No offense taken. You made a great point!"

"Thank you, Derik. And my second point is, well, a tree isn't frozen—it's alive and growing."

Derik nodded. "So, probably not a tree." He began pacing around the crime board, slapping his highlighter on his palm.

"I love watching him walk in circles," smiled Carol.

"You love watching carpet dry," Ava retorted. "Let's admit you don't have high expectations."

"Guys!" shouted Derik. "I think I got it. *Neither man, nor woman, nor beast, nor fowl. Frozen, upon my perch I stand.* It's talking about a statue!"

"Derik! You're a genius," declared Carol. "A statue, on top of something, looking through a telescope."

"That leaves us with three clues: *Worship below, ancients desired my luster,* and *sun forever setting at my back,*" said Ava.

"I'm going to go out on a limb," offered Carol, tapping on her keyboard, "that *ancients desired my luster* has to deal with gold." She stared at the screen to confirm. "Yep, first result in Google is an article titled 'How did gold become desired by ancient civilizations?'"

"So, *ancients desired my luster,*" repeated Derik, thinking out loud. "Is the statue gold, or was whoever the statue represents rich? And, if so, did they worship his wealth?"

"Maybe he's a king?" pondered Ava. "It says *worship below.* Are people bowing down to whoever the statue represents?"

"There wasn't a king here, remember? England had a king when the Puritans first came here: King Charles I. However, the Puritans didn't have a king. At first, they didn't even have a government."

"Maybe it wasn't a real king. Didn't they call Jesus the King of the Jews? Perhaps it's a religious statue," guessed Ava.

"Wait, wait, wait!" said Derik excitedly. "I think you might be on to something."

"Of course, I am," said Ava proudly. "Okay, Derik. Just so we're all clear, tell me what I'm onto."

"*Frozen, upon my perch I stand. Worship below*. Come on, guys," said Derik excitedly. "It's a statue on top of a church!"

"Oh my God," said Carol. "It's the statue of the golden boy on Saint Thomas's Church in Lexington!"

Carol's fingers flew across her keyboard. Seconds later, images of Saint Thomas's Church filled her screen. She jabbed her finger excitedly at her laptop. "Derik's right! Look."

Standing proudly atop the church's steeple stood a statue of a boy holding a golden telescope. "*Neither man, nor woman, nor beast, nor fowl*," whispered Carol. "He's a child, not a man or woman, or a beast or fowl. He's a boy."

"So, what's our next step?" asked Derik.

"I have an idea," offered Ava. "I think we need to look through his telescope to see beyond. You know, to find the next clue."

"That's brilliant, Ava," said Derik, clearly impressed.

"And how do you propose we do that?" asked Carol, a little miffed Ava had stolen her thunder. "The statue's at least a hundred feet up."

"I was gonna suggest we pole vault," Ava replied.

"Tightrope between two trees?" offered Derik. "We'll just need tights and a huge stick."

"Seriously, guys. We're on a time crunch," Carol said humorlessly. "Any ideas?"

"Carol, your dad's an architect. You must know how to get the plans to the church, right?" asked Ava.

"Yeah, I can use my dad's login at the Local Department of Buildings. They'll have the building plans for the church. The problem is…," Carol paused in her typing, "…even if we get on top of the church, we still have to scale the steeple."

"Don't they have ladders on those things? You know, like, attached to them?" asked Derik.

Carol navigated back to the page with the pictures of Saint Thomas's Church. There were photographs of the church from about every angle, but none appeared to show a ladder attached to the steeple.

"I think we can assume," said Carol, "that there's not a ladder."

"All right, tiny issue," acknowledged Ava. "But I think I've got a solution. We're just gonna need some rope, mad cowboy skills, and a lot of luck."

5
SAINT THOMAS'S CHURCH

"That's a long way up," gulped Derik.

He shaded his eyes with the edge of his hand. The golden boy loomed high above them, perched atop a majestic octagonal spire and radiating like a golden god against the blue backdrop of a cloudless sky.

"And," he added, his voice filled with disappointment, "no ladder."

"Derik, did you oversell us on your climbing skills?" teased Ava.

"No, I got it," he squeaked unconvincingly.

"Okay," said Carol. "According to the building plans, the access door to the ceiling is through a door in the balcony. From there, we make our way to the front of the church and into the tower."

"And I suppose we're just going to waltz into the church and climb up the steeple?" asked Derik.

"No," smiled Carol. "Desperate times call for desperate measures. We're going to spoof the church receptionist, Mrs. Florence Weatherby, and then we'll waltz into the church."

"Spoofing? Never mind—I probably don't want to know," said Derik, his excitement quickly devolving into anxiety.

***

The trio crept silently behind the behemoth boxwood bushes that bordered the church, coming to a stop when they reached the cement steps that led into the main entrance.

"So, again, I ask," whispered Derik, "how do we get in?"

"You see those two white doors?" Carol pointed helpfully. "That's how we're getting in. Just follow my lead."

Derik smacked his forehead. "Please tell me that you have a plan that involves more than waltzing."

"I'd prefer we sashay into the church," added Ava. "It's got more attitude."

"Listen, I need you two to focus," Carol admonished. "I'm going to call Mrs. Weatherby, the church receptionist, and pretend like I'm their FedEx driver. No, no, no," snapped Carol, shushing Ava. "I can see your lips moving—let me finish. I'm using an iPhone App that lets me spoof my call, so it looks like it's coming from FedEx."

Derik hung his head like he was about to be sick. "I'm going to be in prison until I'm eighty."

Carol rolled her eyes and continued. "I'll tell her I have a delivery at the side door and I'm locked out. According to the building plans, it will take her about twenty seconds to walk to the door. She'll open it, look around, and then return to her desk, bewildered.

"While she is away from her desk, we go in the front door, down the hallway to the left, and up the stairs to the balcony. Good enough for now, or do you want me to draw a picture?"

"Good enough," replied Derik sheepishly.

"Pfft. You give in too easily," scoffed Ava. "I would've demanded the picture. Her artwork is remedial at best."

"Your artwork is so bad, they created erasers," Carol volleyed back, tapping the spoof app on her phone.

"That made absolutely zero sense," said Ava.

"Because erasers didn't exist until you started creating artwork. Get it? So they created erasers...?"

"Please," sighed Ava, waving at Carol's phone. "Focus on what you do best, and let me handle the humor department."

Carol typed *FedEx* and then a random number into the spoof app. Then, she smiled. "I'm going to type in the number for the church and press Call. Cross your fingers."

Florence Weatherby answered on the second ring. "Hi, Mrs. Weatherby," Carol began in her most professional-sounding tone. "This is Jill with FedEx. I'm parked at your side door. I have an important delivery for, um, Pastor Martin. Could you please come sign for it? It's marked urgent delivery."

"Certainly," Florence agreed. "I'll be right there."

"Thank you so much, Mrs. Weatherby. I truly appreciate it."

Carol patiently counted out five seconds, then said, "Let's go."

The trio quickly climbed up the side of the steps and clambered over the white wooden railings onto the porch. Carol took in a deep breath, grabbed the door handle, and slowly opened the front door of the church. She poked her head inside and looked around.

"She's gone," Carol whispered, pointing to an empty desk. "Come on."

The trio scurried down a narrow hallway toward the back of the church until they reached a door with a sliver of rectangular glass above the handle. The word *Balcony* was painted in black at the top of the door.

Ava, Carol, and Derik slipped through the door and quickly hustled up the stairs to the second floor, with Carol leading the pack. The stairs ended abruptly onto a narrow landing. Carol gently pulled open the door to the balcony.

"Pretty church," whispered Ava, looking down from the balcony into the sanctuary.

"We'll sightsee later," said Carol softly, stopping in front of an unmarked door. "This is how we get to the steeple." She twisted the doorknob. "Locked. Kind of expected that."

"Is there another way to the steeple?" whispered Derik.

"No, this is it—unless you plan on scaling the side of the building."

"Well, we can't say we didn't try," insisted Derik.

"It's not a problem." Ava winked at Carol conspiratorially. "I got a key to this door from the library." Ava pulled a plastic library card from her pocket.

Carol stared. "You're not going to—"

Ava leaned forward and pushed her library card between the door and the frame and slid it downward next to the doorknob. She rotated the card upward, then pushed down. "Almost there," she whispered. She bent the card toward the door handle and jiggled the doorknob. Seconds later, the door swung open.

"Where did you learn how to do that?" asked Derik.

"Ironically, the same place I got this card," smiled Ava. "The library."

Carol reached into her backpack and pulled out a black stocking cap with a LED light attached to the front.

"If you pull out a ninja suit and a sword, I'm outta here," groaned Derik.

"Wow. Looks like a massive attic," whispered Ava, ducking under a tangle of boards arching upward.

"Smells like a giant attic too," declared Derik, clawing a spiderweb from his face.

"Just be careful," insisted Carol, walking along the beams. "We don't want to break through the ceiling."

"Do you really think we could break through?" asked Derik, his eyes as big as saucers.

"Don't know," answered Carol. "Don't wanna find out." Moments later, Carol held up her arm and made a fist, the universal sign for stop. "We need to be as quiet as mice up here," she whispered. "That's the tower." Carol pointed to a square wooden room the size of a small shed. "It's right above the main entrance to the church, where Mrs. Weatherby sits. So, not a sound."

"Yeah," nodded Ava. "I have a feeling Mrs. Weatherby is a little ticked off right now."

Ava and Derik nodded and followed Carol into the entrance to the tower. Sunlight poured inside from four large, circular windows. A narrow wooden ladder nailed to the wall rose up from the tower to the belfry. Derik hoped that it continued to the tip of the spire.

Ava looked up at the tangled mess of boards crisscrossing above her head. Just the thought of climbing a tiny wooden ladder some forty feet into the air made her nauseous.

"How far do we have to go up?" moaned Ava, feeling lightheaded.

"Up three levels, Aves, until we reach the lantern room. There are six windows there. We'll tie off Derik to a support beam, and from there he can scale the spire and look through the telescope. Easy-peasy."

"Yeah," gulped Derik. "Easy-peasy. Are you sure this is the only way? I mean, I could fall."

"Yes, and you're not going to fall," assured Carol. "We're going to secure you to a ceiling beam. They've been here for two hundred years. You'll be fine."

"Says the person who's *not* going to be dangling, like, one hundred feet up in the air."

"I'll go first," said Carol. "Ava, you follow me, and Derik, you bring up the rear."

Carol took one last look up and then began climbing the ladder, which groaned and shuddered as if being awoken from a century-long slumber.

Ava didn't look up nor down. She simply climbed up one rung at a time, staring directly in front of her. It wasn't until Carol said "You made it" that she realized she had reached the top.

"I think you would have continued climbing until you reached the moon," laughed Carol.

"Yeah," agreed Ava. Shaking, she slowly placed a foot on the floor of the lantern room and then peeled her fingers one by one from the ladder. "If I don't begin breathing again in a few minutes, please let me know."

"You did great," smiled Carol, as Derik stepped onto the circular wooden floor beside Ava.

Four giant spotlights, angled north, east, south, and west, were mounted to the center of the floor. Ava knelt in front of one of the giant spotlights and traced the shape of a bat into the dust on the lens.

"Ava!" hissed Carol, making her jump. "What are you doing?"

"Nothing. Just admiring the artistry of these old-timey spotlights. They're amazing."

Carol narrowed her eyes. "Let's focus, guys."

The lantern room had six windows, each about four feet tall and two feet wide. Narrow slats of wood extended widthwise across the windows, dividing each window into four panes of glass.

Derik pressed his forehead against the glass and looked down to the street some seventy feet below. He shook his head. One mistake, and he would plummet to his death.

6
I'M FALLING FOR YOU

The trio painstakingly removed the four panes of glass from the window that faced a thicket of woods at the back of the church.

Derik leaned through the opening and looked below. A tiny wooden border about the width of a shoebox encircled the perimeter outside the lantern room. His eyes traveled from the tiny ledge down to the ground. He regretted telling the girls that he climbed all the time with his dad.

"How is it out there?" asked Carol, seeing the concerned look on Derik's face.

"The woodwork is really old. Hopefully it will support my weight. The good thing is…," he knelt and opened his backpack, "…there's little or no wind blowing out there."

He reached in his pack and removed a fifty-foot braided nylon climbing rope and then a thick black belt with two thick loops dangling from it.

"What the heck is that?" asked Ava. "Looks like those weird outfits the Germans wear during Oktoberfest."

"It's a climbing harness," said Derik proudly, "used by professional climbers."

"Oh," replied Ava, enthused. "It's lovely."

"At least *try* to hide your jealousy," he said, putting a leg through each loop and then pulling the harness up and over his hips.

25

He removed a clasp, attached it to the front of the harness, and then secured the rope with a figure-eight knot.

"I'm impressed," said Carol.

"You can put that on my gravestone," mumbled Derik as he threw the other end of the rope over a massive wooden joist and tied it off.

"If I were a climber," stated Ava, "and I fell to my death, I would just like one word on my tombstone: *Ahhhhh*, with each *h* getting tinier and tinier."

"All right. On that note," he said, stepping backward through the window onto the narrow ledge, "I'm off to wrangle a statue."

Derik stood outside the window, his feet splayed apart, balancing on the ledge that skirted the perimeter. He slowly fed the rope through his harness, laying back gradually. Carol leaned out the window and handed Derik another rope.

"Thanks," said Derik, his voice a thin whisper.

Carol fought the urge to say, *You got this*, or give him some token thought of encouragement. The truth of the matter was, Derik was suspended from a beam in an old tower seventy feet above the earth. *If he fell…* She pushed the thought out of her head and backed away from the window, letting him focus.

The golden statue gleamed in the sunlight—ten feet above Derik. *Ten feet*, thought Derik. *I can do this*. He locked the rope that held him in place, then checked it again. He would need both hands free to lasso the statue.

Derik willed his fingers from around the rope. A wave of vertigo rushed through his body. "Breathe," he whispered.

"Breathe." His heart pulsed so hard he could feel it in his neck. He felt woozy, and his vision began to blur. Just as he was about to give up and tell the girls that he was sorry but couldn't do it, he heard the soft, calming words of his father in his head:

Breathe in through your nose, count to four, out through your mouth, count for eight. In through your nose, count to four, out through your mouth.

Derik closed his eyes and followed his dad's breathing pattern. He felt the beating of his heart slow. His mind was clearing. He opened his eyes and focused on the statue. He was ready.

Derik gathered the rope in his left hand in loose rings. Carol had tied a tight lasso at the other end, securing it with duct tape so it would remain open. Hopefully, this would make roping the statue easier. He whipped his right arm in a circle and released the rope; it soared through the air, completely missing the statue.

"Not bad, not bad," said Derik, giving himself a pep talk. "A little more to the left."

Derik maneuvered his body, swung his arm in a circle, and sent the rope arching skyward. Gravity returned the favor and sent the rope back to him, smacking him in the face.

Inside the lantern room, Ava and Carol paced anxiously. "We need to be thinking," insisted Ava. "What if this doesn't work? What's our plan B? What about the rest of the riddle? We could be working on that."

"I'm proud of you. Usually you would be pacing around the room asking, 'What's my motivation?' But, I digress. I must admit, I hate it when you're the voice of reason."

Ava stretched her arms open wide, about to embrace the praise cast upon her, reveling in her moment, when she saw Carol's eyes fly open in self-realization.

"I take that back." Carol smiled wickedly. "You're the voice of reason, *only* because I'm a great teacher."

"Oh! Oh, no," snapped Ava. "First, I was never your student. Secondly, you have problems accepting the fact that I bested you with my freakishly sporadic gift of intellect."

"Ahem," said a voice from the window. "Sorry to disturb your highly entertaining argument, but I'd like to show you the golden fish I just hooked."

"You roped the statue?" exclaimed Carol.

"Like Wonder Woman and her magic lasso!" Derik exclaimed proudly.

"Great," laughed Ava. "While you're up there, see if you can get the truth out of him."

"Did you say Wonder Woman?" asked Carol.

"I meant like a cowboy, roping a ferocious cow, with big horns—"

"And a bell?" offered Ava.

"Whatever. I just wanted to tell you I'm on my way up."

"Great job, Derik," said Carol, leaning out the window. "Good luck."

"It's not luck," said Derik, running the rope through a clasp on his belt and securing it in place. "This is skill. All skill."

7
I SEE YOU

Derik cautiously tested each foothold as he climbed the steeple. Progress was painfully slow. *This isn't a race,* he reminded himself. Sweat poured down his face and into his eyes. He turned his head and wiped the perspiration from his forehead onto his shoulder. If the salty sweat wasn't distracting enough, he was also being blinded by the sunlight reflecting off the golden statue.

Finally, after what felt like an eternity, Derik's fingers wrapped around the ankle of the golden boy. "Gotcha," he whispered, pulling himself up onto the small circular platform the statue was mounted to.

Derik slowly stood, clinging to the statue's shoulder. He took a moment to gaze out over the town of Lexington, a view he knew he would never have again. Slowly, he worked his way around to the front of the golden figure. The face had been created in splendid detail. Golden curls atop a round, innocent face. Eyes filled with wonder, lips pursed as if he were about to speak.

Derik's eyes fell upon the telescope. It was of simple design, reminding Derik of the toy telescope he had as a child. Derik crouched and tilted his head to look through the eyepiece.

Nothing. Solid black. He looked again. *Maybe,* he thought. He twisted the eyepiece. There was a soft click from inside the telescope. His heart jumped. Twisting his head again, he looked through the eyepiece.

The number *38* appeared, floating in space as if tiny ghosts at the end of the telescope. Beneath it, a simple message: *North 3,043 paces.*

Derik clung to the statue and fished his phone out of his pocket. He texted *38, North 3,043 paces* to Carol. He cocked his head and listened. He could hear the *thwap, thwap* sound of a helicopter approaching.

Great. What if it's a police chopper? thought Derik. He pocketed his phone, turned toward the statue, and smiled. "Thank you, golden boy." He checked the sky once more; he could see the chopper clearly now. It looked like a massive green-and-black dragonfly, and it was heading directly toward the church.

What the heck is he doing? Derik kicked off backward from the circular platform and began repelling down the steeple. The helicopter came to a stop, hovering about twenty feet above the statue. Derik's feet had just reached the top of the lantern room's window when a thick yellow rope was flung from the chopper. Moments later, a figure dressed in all black slid down, landing perfectly beside the statue.

Derik hung suspended in space, his mouth agape. *What is happening?*

The figure in black twisted its head, looked inside the telescope, and then tapped something into its watch. Derik didn't need to guess what it was the individual was typing—he already knew.

The figure stood and then looked down. A smile crept over her face. She turned and gave a thumbs-up to the helicopter. Then, the woman wrapped her legs around the rope military-style and ascended into the bottom of the chopper, and vanished inside.

Church staff and neighbors were beginning to run into the church courtyard. Just like the mysterious woman, Derik had to disappear, and *now*! He pushed off hard, releasing rope through his hand simultaneously, and with one giant swing he flung himself into the window. Ava and Carol caught him before he crashed into the spotlights.

They rushed to the window and looked out, just in time to see the helicopter disappearing over the woods.

"I think we just got outdone by James Bond," exclaimed Ava.

"More like James Blonde," said Derik, slipping out of his harness. "That was a woman with blonde hair. A beautiful woman," he gushed.

"I'm sure she wasn't all that beautiful," huffed Carol. She glanced out the window. A small crowd had gathered and was pointing at the steeple. "Guys," said Carol urgently. "We gotta act like Houdini and vanish!"

Poof!

8
THE LOCAL NEWS

Ava, Carol, and Derik ducked into a booth at Nacho Taco, about two blocks from the church, and discussed the issue at hand.

"So, obviously," continued Carol, "they have more resources than us. I mean, a helicopter and some ninja woman."

"Yeah, that's fine," said Ava, taking a bite of her taco. "We're just gonna have to step up our game."

"I mean, who slides out of a helicopter onto a church?" Carol muttered.

"Probably Jillian Steele," said Derik between bites.

"Wait, you know her? Are you fraternizing with the enemy?" snapped Carol.

"Easy," said Derik. He nodded toward the television behind the soda bar.

There she was, still dressed in her black stretchy suit. A headful of blonde hair with golden streaks graced her head, which was also graced by a tan face, her eyebrows expertly plucked to look like miniature arches.

"No one's teeth are that white," pointed out Carol.

"Great observation." Ava scooted out of her seat, grabbed the remote off the counter, and pressed the volume button.

"Fans of my show, *Expedition Miraculous*, Wednesday nights at seven," she said, winking at the camera, "know that I always find the treasure."

The male reporter grinned so hard it must have hurt. He was obviously enamored by her. "Have you solved any of the riddles yet?"

"Oh, yes. It won't take long to break through this cryptic puzzle."

"Any little *tidbits* you want to share with our viewers?"

"Sorry." She smiled. "A treasure hunter never reveals her clues."

"A treasure hunter never reveals her clues," mocked Carol. She grabbed the remote from Ava's hand and flicked off the television.

"Hey," said a group of mechanics from the service station next door, clearly annoyed that Carol cut the interview short.

"Television will rot your brain. Read a book!" yelled Carol.

"Great," moaned Ava. "My parents take our cars to their shop."

"Sorry." Carol flicked the television back on, navigated to the guide screen, and opened the Home Shopping Network. A woman was gushing over a rainbow-colored crochet purse. "Satisfied?"

Ava snapped up the remote and marched over to the mechanics. "Here, guys," she said, sliding the remote onto the counter. "Sorry about my friend."

"It's okay, kid," said one of the mechanics, fishing his phone out of his pocket. "I'm gonna get one of those purses for my wife."

"Tasteful," smiled Ava. "She'll love it." Ava slid back into her booth. "Look, we can't get distracted by ninja lady."

"Jillian Steele," clarified Derik.

"Not helpful, Derik. She's busy promoting her show and getting press. We need to pretend like she doesn't exist and do what we do best," insisted Carol.

"Kind of hard, when she's literally dropping out of the sky on top of us," countered Ava.

"What's actually going on here? I've never seen anyone rattle you like this," said Derik with a bewildered look on his face.

"It's that someone like her doesn't deserve the money. Flying around in her helicopter in her stretchy clothes…."

"And then," Carol continued, "there's people like Kaitlyn who work hard for every penny they earn." She shook her head. "I was gonna wait to ask you guys, but—"

"You want to give the reward money to Kaitlyn," finished Ava, grabbing her friend's hand.

"Yeah," nodded Carol. "For London. She'd be able to get the cochlear implant and hear."

Ava smiled. "I was gonna suggest the same thing."

"I think that's an incredible idea," said Derik. "Let's do this for London!"

"Let's do it for London," chorused Ava and Carol.

The trio jumped as the television remote slid to a stop in the middle of the table. Ava, Carol, and Derik looked up in unison.

"I'm Bob. I recognize you," the man said, pointing a finger permanently stained with grease. "Your parents bring their cars into the shop."

"Yes, sir," nodded Ava. "My parents said you're fair and honest, and you don't overcharge."

"Well," smiled the man, running his hand through his closely shaved silvery hair, "tell your parents I said thank you."

"I will."

Bob shifted his weight and awkwardly shoved his hands in his pockets. "Not that I was listening to your conversation," he offered in his thick, gravelly voice, "but I *know* Kaitlyn. You're talking about the hairdresser on Elm Street, right?"

"Yes," said Carol, scrunching her brow, confused as to where this conversation was going.

"Kaitlyn's a good kid, and a good mom," he paused, staring out into the parking lot.

He looked out the window for so long everyone at the table turned to see if something was going on outside. When he spoke again, everyone jumped.

"Don't you worry about that fancy lady on the television. Word is, her series is about to be cancelled. She's doing everything she can to get some publicity."

"Whoa," said Ava. "Thank you for the info."

"My pleasure. Have a nice day, kids," said Bob as he turned and walked toward the door.

"Did you hear that? That would explain the grand entrance with the helicopter and the promotional spot on the news," said Derik.

Carol nodded and clasped her hands. "It also means that she's going to be desperate to win this contest."

"And desperate people do desperate things," agreed Ava.

"Exactly," said Carol, grabbing her phone. "Let's figure out this next clue!"

9
CAPTAIN PARKER

"So, we have two clues," declared Carol, "the number 38 and then North 3,043 paces."

"The North 3,043 paces part is pretty straightforward," declared Derik. "Maybe the number 38 is a house or an apartment?"

"Or a post office box," suggested Ava.

"Why don't we calculate the distance from the church heading north, and we'll see what's there?" offered Carol.

"Good plan," agreed Ava. She grabbed her phone from her pocket. "So, first…," she slid her finger across her screen, "Google says four hundred paces equal one thousand feet."

"There are 5,280 feet in a mile," rattled off Carol.

"Perfect. Thank you, Big Brain. So, according to my calculator, it's a smidge under a mile and a half. We need to go to the church and travel north for a mile and a half!"

"There's a much easier way." Carol opened a map application on her phone and zoomed in on the church. "Here's Saint Thomas's Church. I'll drop a location marker at the front of the steeple, and…," she took her index finger and drew a straight line north across the screen, "…I'll stop right here at the 1.5 mile mark and drop another location marker."

"And where is it?" Derik asked excitedly.

"One second." Carol zoomed in. "It looks like the middle of Massachusetts Avenue."

"Is there anything near there that could be a clue? Anything with the number 38?" asked Ava.

"What's that clump of trees right there?" asked Derik, pointing to her screen.

"Not sure." Carol clicked the plus button and zoomed in even more. "It's another statue. The map app has it tagged as the Minuteman Statue."

"Minuteman Statue," repeated Ava as she searched on her phone. "Google says that the statue honors Captain John Parker, commander of the Lexington Patriot army. The statue was unveiled by his grandson, Charles Parker, on April 19, 1900. Whoa. It also says," she continued, "forty thousand people attended the unveiling."

"Okay," said Derik. "We need to think this through. We have these clues because we solved the first riddle."

"So did the *Expedition Miraculous* woman," added Carol.

"True," agreed Derik. "So we can pretty much surmise that they are going to figure out the clues from the telescope just as fast as we did. My point is, just because we've been given a location, it doesn't mean we've solved the second clue. We figured out the location of the golden statue, right? But we still had to figure out that we had to look through the telescope to get the next clue."

"That's true," agreed Ava. "Carol, hit us with the second riddle."

"Sure," said Carol, swiping her finger across her phone. "*Where the road divides, stands a warrior in repose. Beneath his shadow, the living mirror lies. Written within, by neither feather nor pen. Without it, life would die.*"

"You see?" explained Derik quietly. "If we didn't have the clue from the telescope, there's a good chance we would never have figured out that it's talking about the Minuteman statue."

"Yeah, true," nodded Carol. "And the location is only half of it. We know that where the road divides is the intersection at Bedford Street and Massachusetts Avenue. We also know that the warrior who stands in repose is Captain Parker, but that's it."

"We still have that weird cryptic passage," added Derik. "I think our best bet is to figure out the living mirror part that's beneath his shadow."

"Well, there's only one way to do that," replied Carol.

"I agree," said Derik, already scooting across his seat. "We need to get to that statue!"

***

Ava, Carol, and Derik hurried across Massachusetts Avenue into Lexington Common, a triangular-shaped park filled with historical markers and tourists.

Ava stopped in front of a granite rock and read the plague aloud. "It was here," she gestured broadly, "on April 19th in 1775 that an army of 250 British soldiers confronted eighty men from the Lexington Militia under the command of Captain John Parker. He's famous for telling his men, 'Stand your ground,'" Ava emphasized the point throwing her fist into the air. "'Don't fire unless fired upon, but if they mean to have a war let it begin here.'"

"Nicely read Ava," smiled Derik. "You'd make an incredible tour guide."

"Thank you, I enunciate well...it's part of my charm."

Carol carefully surveilled the Lexington Battle Green, looking for anyone who appeared suspicious or had blonde hair and was wearing a black stretchy outfit. Her shoulders relaxed when her brief reconnaissance came up empty for enemy spies.

"The statue's up there," said Ava, pointing to a soldier standing atop a slab of granite surrounded by a small cluster of tourists.

Captain Parker stood proudly atop a small mountain of field stones. The bronze statue, now patina, showed a young man, his shirt sleeves rolled up over his forearms, with a rifle in his hands resting across his thigh. His face was calm, yet powerful, ready to face whatever challenges came his way.

"It's a beautiful statue," said Carol, mingling in with a group of tourists posing for selfies and taking pictures.

"I wonder what he would say if he could talk," mused Ava. "I mean, think how much history he's seen. Horse-drawn carriages, cars, airplanes...."

"Guys, now's not the time to get all philosophical," interrupted Derik, spreading his hands.

"Sorry," agreed Ava. "I hate to say it, but Carol might be rubbing off on me."

"Great. Maybe they can make a Hallmark movie about your friendship," Derik retorted.

"All right, all right," whispered Carol, ushering them out of earshot of the tourists. "We need to look for anything related to the number 38 and…," she paused for a moment, recalling the clues, "…a living mirror beneath his shadow."

"And for something not written by feather nor a pen. Oh, and also, without it, life would die," added Ava.

The trio searched the entire statue and all of the rocks that made up the base, but they could find nothing with the number 38 in sight.

"Maybe there are thirty-eight rocks, and that was a clue as to the location of the statue," said Ava, grasping at straws.

"We're not really counting rocks," groaned Derik. "Come on."

Ava shrugged, not giving up. "Maybe he was thirty-eight when he died?"

"No, he was forty-six," said Carol from behind the statue.

"I don't know. How about we look for the other clues? Then, maybe the number 38 will make sense."

Carol joined Ava and Derik at the front of the statue.

"I don't see anything that could be a living mirror," moaned Ava. "The man is surrounded by rocks and flowers."

"He's surrounded by plants. Maybe without plants people would die. You know, food? Oxygen?" offered Derik.

"They're flowers, and I don't think they are edible," Carol disagreed.

"How about love? The flowers could represent love. Without love, you would die. And something that isn't written by a feather nor a pen—it could be written in the stars. A romantic clue," gushed Ava, swooping her arms.

"Hallmark," repeated Derik. "A lifelong career is waiting for you."

"Okay," groaned Carol. "Ava's losing her mind. Let's shoot some video footage and take some pictures. Then, we'll head back to The Lair. Maybe something will click."

10
FLOWER INJUSTICE

Ava flicked on the projector hooked to her laptop. "I present, Captain Parker," announced Ava, gesturing at the image of the statue projected on the wall.

"Yep, he still looks the same," said Derik. "Tall, dark, and green."

"That's patina," clarified Carol. "The copper turns green over time. Just like the Statue of Liberty, which used to be brown like a giant penny."

"Oh, cool," said Derik. "I should have known that, my dad owning Charter Bank, and all."

"So, Captain Parker's statue used to be brown?" asked Ava.

"Pretty sure," replied Carol. Her fingers clicked across the keyboard. "Yep, here's an actual newspaper clipping. Says here that the statue was made from bronze and was originally a functioning drinking trough for horses, cattle, and dogs but has since been converted into a planter."

Carol paused. "The trough was filled with water," she said softly, as if that explained everything.

"That's right," nodded Ava, "for horses and dogs to drink from."

"A living mirror. Don't you see?" she said, looking excitedly at Ava. "Water reflects things, like a mirror," she gushed.

43

"And without it, life would die," added Derik.

"You think the answer to the clue is inside that trough thingy? Beneath a hundred pounds of dirt?" asked Ava incredulously.

"It all makes sense," insisted Carol.

"Amazing. I don't know how you do it," praised Derik, shaking his head. "Carol, you're a genius!"

"Don't lay it on too thick," warned Ava. "Her Hello Kitty headband can barely fit around her massive head as it is."

"You're just jealous," chided Carol.

"No, but I'll tell you what I am. I'm pretty sure your headband is actually a wristband. Think about it."

Carol was about to reply when she stopped and thought about it. "Hmm, I bet that's why I've been getting so many headaches."

Ava shot her a *Ya think?* look.

"Ahem," said Derik, staring at the projected image of the statue on the wall.

"What?" asked Carol abruptly. "I mean, yes? You had something to say?"

"I was wondering, how do you propose we empty out a bathtub-sized basin filled with flowers and dirt in the middle of Lexington without being seen?"

Carol pushed her chair back and joined Derik, studying the statue. "Well...it is surrounded by bushes."

"And a streetlight, and houses, and traffic. Need I continue?" asked Ava.

"We seem to spend a lot of time in bushes," commented Derik.

"I have a plan," offered Carol, a smile slowly spreading across her face. "We're going to need trash bags, shovels, and a lot of luck."

"And bail money for the destruction of private property," added Ava.

***

Ava, Carol, and Derik pedaled furiously through the back streets of Lexington. It was 1 a.m. A small weather front had moved in, bringing with it rain and gusting winds. Ava breathed in deeply; she loved the smell of the rain, the way the wind playfully tussled her hair. Maybe Carol's plan wasn't going to be so terrible after all. What could possibly go wrong?

Carol brought her bike to a sliding stop just inside the tree line of Lexington Common. Ava and Derik pulled up alongside her.

"Why are we stopping?" asked Ava, pulling back the hood of her hoodie. "Did you see something?"

"No, just being cautious," said Carol quietly. "There's a wall of bushes behind the statue. I think we should hide the bikes there."

"We should write a book called *A Private Investigator's Guide to Shrubbery*. Best bushes to hide behind, what makes a good shrub...," Derik suggested.

"I think you're wearing off on him," said Carol sadly.

"One of my proudest moments," beamed Ava.

"I wish that streetlight wasn't right there," said Derik, nodding toward the light that illuminated the small island of grass and rock that Captain Parker stoically guarded.

"Nothing we can do about that. We'll just need to be super alert," replied Carol.

Derik nodded silently in agreement. Without another word, they pedaled through the wet grass to the back of the statue, where they ditched their bikes behind a row of bushes.

With their bikes safely hidden, the trio, dressed in dark hoodies and sweatpants, crawled on hands and knees around the rocky base of the statue, hiding behind the large trough overflowing with peonies and irises.

"Okay," whispered Carol, pulling on a pair of gloves. "We're going to have to be fast and furious."

"I prefer *Gone in 60 Seconds*, if we're naming movies," whispered Derik.

"Someone needs to hit the reset button on him," moaned Carol. "Listen, flowers in these two bags, and dirt in these. If anyone comes—"

"We know," interrupted Ava. "This isn't our first rodeo— especially for him." She nudged Derik's shoulder. "He's lassoed a golden statue."

Derik beamed. "I'm so amazing."

"And modest," added Ava, uprooting flowers by the handful.

Ava and Carol made quick work of the flowers, carefully placing them in the trash bags, making sure not to damage them, while Derik kept watch. Aside from a police cruiser, a couple of cars, and an occasional late-night dog walker, the streets remained empty.

"Derik, do you think you can keep an eye on things and dig at the same time?" whispered Carol. "There's a crazy amount of dirt in this thing."

"Not a problem," answered Derik softly. "I'm itching to get my hands dirty."

Thirty minutes later, Ava's fingers were scraping across the bottom of an empty trough. "That's it," she whispered excitedly. "We're officially dirt-free."

Carol unfolded a trash bag and laid it across the top of the empty basin to hide the glow of her flashlight. Like a mechanic peering under the hood of a car, she raised the edge of the trash bag and stuck her head inside the planter.

Ava and Derik kept an eye out for cars and passersby.

"Anything?" asked Derik softly, unable to contain himself any longer.

"Maybe," said Carol excitedly. "There is definitely something here. Hand me a bottle of water."

Derik unfastened his backpack and grabbed a bottle of water. "Here," he said, handing the bottle to Carol. "It's Smartwater. I thought we could use all the help we could get."

Ava nodded her head in agreement and chuckled. She liked the way Derik thought. "I forgive you for the 'I'm so amazing' comment," she whispered.

Carol pulled her head from the basin, a huge smile on her face. "We've got another clue and another number!"

"What is it?" asked Ava excitedly.

"Yes, what is it?"

Ava, Carol, and Derik's heads jerked upward, their mouths dropping open. It was Jillian Steele.

"Evil!" screeched Carol, jumping to her feet and pointing. "What do you want?"

"Fame, success, perfect bangs...you know, what every woman wants."

"You know what I mean," hissed Carol. "I'm not telling you a thing. Remember, treasure hunters never reveal their clues." Carol shook her hair and giggled, the way Jillian had done on television.

"Oh, darling, you're going to tell me everything, or Frank, my cameraman...," cued by her introduction, a thin man dressed in a black *Expedition Miraculous* T-shirt and skinny jeans appeared from behind the statue, "...is going to make a call to the...what town is this?" she asked, looking around. "Oh, yes, the Lexington Police Department. Seems like we have video of you three vandalizing a historical landmark."

"We're not vandalizing a historical landmark. We simply noticed that the flowers were improperly planted. We're correcting a flower injustice," clarified Ava.

"Well, Frank, looks like we're gonna have to make that call," said Jillian, putting on a pouty face. Frank placed his camera on the ground and fished his phone out of his ultra-tight jeans.

Ava was about to tell Carol it would take the man a week to get his phone out of his pants pocket, but Carol was already talking again.

"Stop," snapped Carol. "I'll give you the clue."

"Oh? I knew we could come to an amicable agreement," smiled Jillian. "So, what's the clue? No, wait!" she said, holding up her hand. "This is embarrassing, but the truth is, I don't really trust you. Why don't you *show* me the clue?"

Ava and Derik stepped aside to let Jillian pass by. "You have to crouch and look at the bottom of the basin with a flashlight," said Carol, trembling with anger.

"Frank, give me your T-shirt. I'm not kneeling on this filthy ground. These Lululemon leggings cost a fortune." Jillian pulled a hairband off her wrist and quickly pulled her wild, flowing blonde hair into a messy ponytail.

Carol leaned over the basin beside her and shined the flashlight at the bottom. Carved into the stone was the number 17, and below it were the words *Flora F.*

"Flora F," said Jillian, leaning back onto her heels. "What do you think it means?"

"How would I know?" asked Carol incredulously. "I obviously just found the clue."

"Well," said Jillian, tossing Frank his shirt. "Since you've been such a big help…," she pushed her lips out like she was placating a toddler, "we'll give you five minutes before we call the cops. Starting now!"

"You said if we gave you the clues—" raged Ava.

"Oh," interrupted Jillian, a sly smile appearing on her face. "Rule number two: Never trust another treasure hunter. And if you want to know another secret—we'll call it number three: Treasure hunters will do whatever they have to do to win, and that usually means getting rid of the competition, like you, you, and especially you," she smiled, poking Carol's shoulder. "Toodles," she called out as she walked away.

Ava, Carol, and Derik shared a look. They were enraged, but they knew that they only had five minutes before Frank called the cops—that was, if they could trust them to wait five minutes.

They dropped to the ground and began filling the trough as fast as they could. Ava pulled the flowers from the trash bag and began replanting them. "Sorry," she repeated over and over as she shoved their roots into the soil.

Carol grabbed another trash bag and dropped the small shovels and other used bags inside. She balled it up under her arm, just as Derik hissed, "Police!"

"Go!" whispered Ava. "Go!"

The trio slid on their bellies to the back of the statue, slithering to a stop behind the bushes where their bikes were hidden.

A heavyset police officer climbed out of the police cruiser and hitched his pants up. He grabbed a flashlight and flicked it on, playing it across the ground at his feet as he approached the monument.

"As soon as he gets to the front of the statue," whispered Carol, "we bolt."

Ava and Derik nodded and silently climbed onto their bikes. The police officer lumbered along the sidewalk, flickering his light over the statue and the bushes.

"Now!" urged Carol softly, hunching over the handlebars and driving her heel hard against the pedal. Derik and Ava joined Carol, pedaling furiously across Lexington Common, their tires slipping and sliding as they sped across the wet grass.

"Hey, you! Stop!"

Ava whipped her head around; the police officer was bounding toward his cruiser, the light from his flashlight bouncing up and down as he ran. Ava stood on her pedals, pulling her handlebars toward her as she jumped a ditch and tore up a muddy embankment, heading into the woods.

Behind them, they could hear the squeal of tires. The police officer spun the cruiser around; its headlights cut through the darkness like lasers. Blue lights flashing, the police car sped down the road, searching for them.

The path through the woods was twisty and narrow and filled with giant mud puddles that threatened to suck their bikes from under them. But after forty-five minutes of hard pedaling, the group emerged from the woods three miles from the statue, soaking wet and covered in mud, but safe.

II
APPLE ORCHARD

Ava leaned back in the chair, stretched, and yawned. "What is it that you have against sleep? It's 7 a.m."

"We need to get an early start if we're going to win the contest," Carol told her. "Jillian has a massive head start against us now."

"How so?" moaned Ava, resting her forehead in her hands.

"While we were playing hide-and-seek with the police, she was probably back at her hotel room drinking martinis and working on the clues."

The girls turned their heads in unison at the sound of a soft chime. Ava clicked the security icon on her laptop, opening the video feed from the door camera. The camera was completely blocked, except for a massive logo that read Dillard's Donut Shack. "Derik's here," chirped Ava, "and he bears gifts!"

Carol hopped up from her chair and raced to the door. "Donuts," she gushed, taking in a deep breath.

"And *Derik*," said Derik, holding out his hands as if to say, *What gives? I'm here too!* "What's that saying?" asked Derik, turning to Ava. "The way to a man's heart is through his stomach."

"I'm sorry," said Ava. "I can't hear you over that bag of donuts."

Derik glanced at the crime board and noticed Carol had circled the Minuteman clue in red and added the number 17 and the words *Flora F.* "So, did you guys figure out anything new since last night?"

"No," said Ava, taking the bag of donuts from his hand. "We're just getting started." She grabbed a powdered donut filled with strawberry jelly and handed the bag to Carol.

"So," he said, gesturing toward the board. "I'm guessing you looked up the words *Flora F*?"

"Yeah," said Ava. "Flora means flower in Spanish. It's also the name of a million locations and businesses."

"It's a capital letter," said Derik. "So it should be a proper noun, and the way that it was written, it's probably a person's name."

"Yeah, I figured that too," said Carol, munching on a glazed donut. "Thank you, by the way," she offered, holding up half a donut. "Once again, though, there are a zillion people named Flora."

"All right," said Derik, taking a seat beside Carol. "Let's do what we did before: work through the clues, one by one."

"It's what we were about to do, when you distracted us with sugar," smiled Ava, wiggling her eyebrows.

"Okay, I'm gonna read the whole thing through out loud," Derik announced. "Sometimes that helps."

Carol gestured for him to proceed, her mouth too full of donut to speak.

"From my orchard, I place an apple on the mantel above my fire. Hidden in the arch, you will find what you desire. An

orchard of sisters, an intellect, a muse, a teller of little stories, my name but a ruse.... Can I just say I feel like we got ripped off by this last clue? I mean, the first clue said: Walk a gazillion feet, head north, and you'll find what you're looking for. This one's like, good luck...."

A gentle knock interrupted Derik. Ava's mom peeked her head through the doorway. "Sorry, Derik," she smiled, "but I brought you guys some juice."

"How'd you know we needed juice?"

"It's mom voodoo," joked Carol, "don't try to understand."

"I saw Derik walking across the backyard with the donuts from the kitchen window. So, I figured...."

"That's why my mom's an amazing investigative journalist," offered Ava. "She observes, deduces, and then produces."

"Nicely done," said Carol, high-fiving Ava.

"So," said Mrs. Clarke again, placing the juice on a table. "Are these the clues for the contest?"

"Yes, ma'am," said Derik. "We've solved the first two."

"Really?" Ava's mom nodded her approval. "Do you mind?" she asked, motioning to the crime board.

"Not at all," said Carol. "We need all the help we can get."

"So, when I'm investigating a story, I look for a few things. Who is the story about? What is the story about? What doesn't belong? And what makes the story important?"

"Cool, so the first question is: Who is the story about?" asked Ava.

"Yep," smiled Mrs. Clarke. "What components are about the person?"

"Well," offered Ava, "we know that they own an orchard—most likely an apple orchard. The person has a fireplace, where I am guessing they've hidden something."

"They have sisters," added Derik. "And," he paused, "I think it's a woman."

"Hmm," prompted Ava's mom. "Why would you suggest that?"

"The word *muse*," answered Derik tentatively. "Aren't most women described as being a muse?"

"Very good," encouraged Mrs. Clarke. "In Greek history and religion, muses are the inspirational goddesses of literature, science, and the arts."

"She is also a teller of little stories. So, maybe a poet? I'm not sure what she means by *my name but a ruse*," Carol mentioned.

"Think about it, Carol," nudged Mrs. Clark. "What's a ruse?"

"A ruse means to fool or deceive someone." Carol's eyes lit up. "A pseudonym!"

"A what?" asked Ava, looking back and forth from her mom to Carol.

"It's a fictitious name," explained her mom. "Like an author's pen name. J. K. Rowling, the creator of Harry Potter, is a good example. Her real name is Joanne Rowling."

"Oh, cool," said Ava.

"Little tidbit for you," said her mom, "when Joanne wrote *Harry Potter*, her publishers thought that young boys wouldn't want to read a book written by a woman. So, they asked her to use her initials instead."

"So, the person in this clue most likely used a pen name," said Carol excitedly.

"May very well be so. I've got a big story to finish. I'm going to leave you guys to it. Good luck!"

"Thanks, Mom!" yelled Ava as her mom closed the door.

Carol hurried over to the crime board and drew four columns. She gave each a title. *Who, What, Doesn't belong*, and *Important*.

Under *Who*, she wrote, *owns an apple orchard, woman, has sisters, intellect, a muse, a teller of little stories, fictitious name.*

"Okay. Next," Carol said, pointing to the column titled *What*. "What is the story about?"

"It's about a woman who places an apple on the mantel above her fireplace, and there is something hidden there."

"In the *arch* of her fireplace," added Ava.

"Yeah," nodded Derik. "And the rest…," he paused, rereading the clues, "…are hints as to her identity."

"Great," said Carol, writing out their comments on the crime board. "And now, what doesn't belong?"

"I'm not sure that it doesn't belong," suggested Ava, "but the word *orchard* is used twice. And teller of *little stories* just seems weird to me."

"I agree," seconded Derik. "I was just wondering, when it says *an orchard of sisters, an intellect, a muse, a teller of little stories*, if she was describing her sisters or herself. Like, one sister was an intellect, another was a teller of stories…."

"Oh, good point," said Carol, nodding and making a note on the board. "So," she said, turning back to Derik and Ava, "what makes the story important?"

"The fact that she has hidden something that we desire," replied Ava. "It would have to be something that a lot of people desire, because she assumes that it is something that we all desire," she declared. "Like money."

"It's pretty straightforward once it's broken down," agreed Derik. "She gives us clues as to her identity and the location of something hidden. We find out who she is. Then, the rest should be easy."

"All right," agreed Carol. "We've got tons of clues. The word *orchard* seems to be significant—she uses it twice. That can't be a coincidence. Ava, you jump on *apple orchards*. See if you can tie any of the clues to one of the orchards near us."

"On it," replied Ava, clicking away on her laptop.

"Derik, search on *orchard of sisters*, and see if anything pops. I'll try to find a writer who used the pseudonym *Flora F.*"

"There are nine orchards within twenty miles of us," shouted Ava. "I'm opening a separate browser tab for each of their websites."

"Perfect," said Carol. "Let us know if you find anything that even remotely connects it to one of the clues."

The Lair was silent, except for the clicking of keys as the trio put Google through its paces. Carol looked up from her screen at her friends, busily filtering through search results. *I wonder if Jillian is struggling with this one too.*

"Guys, guys," said Derik excitedly, waving Ava and Carol to his laptop. "I found a website called *orchard of sisters*. I went to their *About Us* page on their website—and guess where the idea for their name came from?" He turned his laptop so the girls could see the screen.

"The Orchard House," whispered Carol excitedly.

"Yep," nodded Derik. "And...," he turned his eyes on the screen and read, *"The grounds contained an orchard of forty apple trees and was the home of the famous author, Louisa May Alcott."*

"Louisa May Alcott!" spat Ava. "She wrote *Little Women*, one of my favorite books."

Derik gave her a suspicious sideways glance.

"What was that look?" she asked, smacking him on the back of the head. "Yes, I read."

"A teller of little stories!" continued Carol. "The book, *Little Women*, was all about her sisters!"

"Her house is literally fifteen minutes away from here," said Derik. "In Concord."

"I wonder...." Carol raced over to her laptop and typed *pen names used by Louisa May Alcott*. A huge smiled appeared on her face. "She had two pen names. The first one was A. M. Barnard, and the second...," she paused for dramatic effect, "...Flora Fairfield."

"So, that solves the *Flora F* mystery," declared Ava.

"Says here that she used the name Flora Fairfield to publish a series of poems and little stories in the 1850s," announced Carol. "It also says scholars didn't figure out A. M. Barnard was one of her pseudonyms until 1970—nearly one hundred years after her death."

"Come on, guys," said Derik, jumping to his feet. "Looks like we've got a fireplace to inspect."

12
THE ORCHARD HOUSE

The Orchard House was a simple two-story, brown, slat-wood house, with a bright green door adorned with a lion's head doorknocker. Rows of windows looked out onto Lexington Street. A large brick chimney rose from the center of the house.

Carol smiled, imagining cold winter nights when smoke would be swirling from the chimney, the smell of burning cedar in the air and candles glowing in the windows.

"It's amazing," said Carol, turning to Ava and Derik. "Louisa May Alcott's neighbors were Emerson, Hawthorne, and Thoreau. It's crazy to think about them all being friends."

"Lots of history here," agreed Derik.

"Guys," said Ava, bringing everyone to a halt just outside the gift shop. "Don't you think we need some kind of plan before we go in there? This is a guided tour. They're not just gonna give us free rein of the house." She glanced at Derik. "Yes?" she prompted, noticing his *I gotta an idea* face.

"Facetime," offered Derik, as if that explained everything.

"Go on," urged Carol.

"I'll go on the tour first. I'll put my phone in my pocket like this." He flipped his phone around in his pocket so the camera was barely peeking out. "That way, you guys can hear, and see, everything that goes on in the tour...."

"And figure out what to do," finished Ava. "I like it."

"Me too," agreed Carol. "Try to get a good shot of the fireplace if you can."

"I will," nodded Derik. "Wish me luck." He waved, walking to the side entrance of the house.

"What's that other building?" asked Ava, pointing to a water-stained wooden building that looked like a barn.

"That's the Concord School of Philosophy," explained Carol. "It was founded by Louisa May Alcott's father, Bronson Alcott."

"So, Louisa never had an excuse for being late to school," laughed Ava.

"Nope," agreed Carol. "Plus, her dad was her teacher."

"That's rough."

"Depends. Her dad was pretty controversial for that time period. He taught things that were considered rebellious."

Ava perked up at the words *controversial* and *rebellious*. "I'm listening," she said, giving Carol her full attention.

"Well, for starters, Mr. Alcott was a transcendentalist—"

"Oh, I see what you're doing. You lure me in with words like *rebellious* and *cool*...."

"I never used the word *cool*."

"It was implied. And then, you throw in a word like...." She shifted her feet, trying to remember.

"Transcendentalist?" prompted Carol.

"Exactly. I think you just make up nonsense words to mess with me," insinuated Ava.

"Maybe," teased Carol, "but it's a real word. A transcendentalist believes in the inherent goodness of people and nature. He believed that organized religion and politics corrupted individuals."

Ava gave her a look. "I'm not touching that one. My dad said there are two things you never talk about over dinner: religion and politics."

"Exactly," replied Carol, "but he did, and because his philosophical views were so different than others, he was considered a rebel. He also fought for women's rights and believed in educational equality for all people."

"Okay," nodded Ava. "He does sound like a cool dad. I like the fact that he stood up for what he believed in."

"Plus," added Carol with a smile, "you'll like this. He was big on risk-taking in the classroom. He actually allowed his students to debate him if they didn't agree with what he taught, and he thought that physical activity was just as important as book study."

"I can tell you have a history-crush on this guy. Maybe you could write a stirring composition for him on your bassoon." Ava boosted her voice dramatically: "Ladies and gentlemen, I present to you, a tribute to Bronson in B-flat, by Carol Miller, bassoonist. With Derik Charter on the—"

Carol's phone buzzed in her pocket. "On the phone," Carol finished for Ava with a laugh, as Derik's Facetime invite appeared on the screen.

"Hopefully he remembered to turn his volume down," whispered Ava.

The girls sat down on a bench between the schoolhouse and the Alcott house. A constant flow of tourists passed by, taking pictures and talking excitedly.

Carol rotated her phone horizontally, and Ava scooted in close against her, so she could see the screen. "They're in the kitchen," said Carol softly.

"Are they going to tour the whole house?" asked Ava.

"Most likely," answered Carol.

"I should have packed a lunch. I do my best thinking on a full stomach."

"I count about twelve people in his tour group," said Carol. "Our best bet is to join a group with a lot of people."

"They're going up the stairs," said Ava excitedly. They could hear the tour guide's shrill voice telling people to turn into the room at the top of the stairs and not to touch anything.

The girls watched as Derik walked through a doorway and then into Louisa May Alcott's bedroom. He'd placed his cell phone in his front pocket, so he was pretty much shooting from the hip.

"There's the fireplace," said Carol excitedly.

Derik turned and angled the camera directly at the fireplace. The mantel and sides were painted a creamy white, and just above the opening was a picture of an owl on a branch.

"Louisa loved owls," said a woman's high voice. "The painting here above the fireplace was done by her sister, May. Why do you suppose she painted an owl?"

"She loved owls?" someone replied.

"Good job, Captain Obvious," muttered Ava.

"Well, yes," said the woman. "Louisa loved watching a family of owls that lived in the tree, just outside this window. May also painted the owl because they represent wisdom, and she thought Louisa was absolutely brilliant."

Derik's camera suddenly dropped lower, as if he were crouching down to tie his shoes.

"He's showing us the fireplace," said Carol.

The exterior of the firebox was painted black and was in the shape of a horseshoe. As far as Carol could see, the interior was made of red brick. Derik stood and then slowly turned so the girls could see the interior of the room. Suddenly, the camera arched upward, then down, then swooshed around.

"What the heck is a matter with Derik's hips?" asked Ava.

"I think he's trying to point the camera upward so we can see the rest of the room," snickered Carol, imagining Derik in the room, gyrating his hips.

In the background, they could hear the tour guide talking about Louisa May being a nurse in the American Civil War. "Louisa sometimes wrote twelve to fourteen hours, even though she was very sick from mercury poisoning."

"How did she get mercury poisoning?" asked a male voice.

"Louisa contracted typhoid fever during the war. Back then, there were no antibiotics, and they treated her with a compound that contained mercury. Her health suffered greatly after that."

Ava and Carol heard some murmuring from the people in the room, and then the tour guide's voice again. "Any more questions? No? Okay, if you would follow me across the hall, we'll visit the Alcotts' master bedroom."

"I've gotta hide behind her bed," said Carol. "When everybody leaves the room, I'll drop behind the bed and check the fireplace."

"It's the only place to hide," agreed Ava. "I'll create some kind of distraction to get everyone's attention on me."

"Aves, let me see your phone for a second."

"Okay," said Ava curiously, handing her the phone. "What are you looking for?"

"Not looking for anything. I'm installing a Halloween ringtone app. Here." Carol grinned, giving Ava her phone back.

Carol fished her phone out of her pocket and called Ava. Seconds later, a bloodcurdling scream erupted from Ava's phone.

"Holy moly," cried Ava, jumping up from the bench, slamming her thumb against the end call button.

"How's that?" smiled Carol mischievously.

"Effective," laughed Ava. "Highly effective."

13
SCREAM

Derik paced nervously outside. Ava and Carol had left for the tour fifteen minutes ago. He figured the girls had watched the ten-minute movie that they played at the beginning of the tour and were probably in the living room by now. That was when he saw a tall, blonde woman step out of a black Mercedes. "Jillian," he muttered.

He pulled out his phone and quickly texted *Jillian's here.*

Carol blended into the middle of the tour group as they made their way upstairs. She'd been careful not to make any eye contact with the guide. Ava hung out at the front of the pack, her heart pounding as she readied for her performance.

Carol felt her phone vibrate. She snuck a peak as they were herded into Louisa May Alcott's room. She took in a deep breath. If Jillian saw them, she could ruin everything, and there was no way she could warn Ava.

Ava and Carol's tour guide was an elderly woman with a solid helmet of white hair. She wore blue glasses decorated with little silver flowers and a matching blue dress with a white apron.

She worked Louisa's room like a clock, rattling off details about her bed, her writing desk, the owls, and a bookcase that showcased the *Little Women* book translated into dozens of other languages. She stopped and eyed the fireplace located beside the bedroom door and pointed out the screech owl, painted by Louisa's sister, May.

Ava's heart beat faster; she knew that at any second her phone was gonna erupt into a bloodcurdling scream.

"Okay," said the woman, gesturing toward the door. "Let's move on to the Alcotts' master bedroom."

Just as the elderly guide stepped beside Ava, her phone let loose a horrific scream. Ava didn't need to act surprised; the scream startled her so much she slammed into the doorframe.

Carol crouched and dove beneath Louisa's bed. Her first thought: *When was the last time they dusted?*

Carol gritted her teeth. Ava was getting the tongue-lashing of a lifetime from the tour guide. She could hear Ava apologizing over and over. The woman finally stormed off, her voice tinged with anger, as she led the tour group into the Alcotts' master bedroom.

"Before I start," she could hear the elderly woman saying, "please, young lady, make sure your phone is off."

Carol rolled from beneath the bed and crept to the fireplace. She didn't bother to check the door—at this point there was no turning back. She knelt on the brick hearth and reached up into the firebox.

The clue said in the arch of the fireplace, Carol repeated in her mind. She ran her hand along the inside of the firebox. There was a row of bricks that slightly protruded like a miniature shelf on the inside.

Carol gave each brick a tug. The third brick slid loose into her hand.

"Oh my God," whispered Carol, cradling the brick in her hand. The inside of the brick had been scooped out as if by an ice cream scooper, and inside lay a tiny cylindrical metal tube.

Suddenly, Carol heard the clomping of feet coming up the stairs. It was the next tour group!

Carol shoved the tube in her pocket and had just replaced the brick when the new group began pouring into the room.

She leapt to her feet. "Shoe was untied," she explained, pointing to her sneakers. Without a second thought she turned to leave, throwing up her hands—and then crashing into Jillian.

"Watch where you're going," snapped Jillian, grabbing Carol's wrist. A big smile spread over her face. "Frank," she said, turning. "Look who we've got here." Her eyes dropped to Carol's hands. "Why are your fingers all black?"

"Let go of me!" yelled Carol, ripping her hands free from Jillian's grasp.

Carol moved to step through the doorway, but Jillian blocked her. "I think I need to notify the tour guide that you've stolen something from this room."

"What? I tripped on the hearth when I was leaving. I didn't steal anything."

"I think we'll let them decide."

"You can't keep me in here," hissed Carol angrily.

Jillian turned to the tour guide, now pushing her way through the guests. "This girl was in Louisa May Alcott's room all by herself, and she has what looks like soot all over her fingers."

A young woman with curly brown hair and a heart-shaped face appeared at the top of the steps. *She can't be but nineteen,* thought Carol.

The woman's eyes dropped to Carol's hands and then moved to her face. "What were you doing in this room?" Her voice wasn't accusatory, but it was sharp and to the point.

"I tripped and fell. I was tying my sneaker, trying to hurry up with the other group. I didn't steal anything. I am not a thief."

The elderly woman from Ava's group appeared in the doorway of the Alcotts' master bedroom. She glanced at the young woman. "What's going on, Amy?"

Amy gestured at Carol. "This young lady said she fell and was tying her shoe."

The smile on Jillian's face grew even larger when she saw Ava in the other tour group.

"These two," offered Jillian, pointing at Ava and Carol, "are already wanted by the police for vandalizing a historic monument in Lexington."

"What are you talking about?" yelled Ava.

"Frank," said Jillian to her assistant, "show them your phone."

All eyes turned to Frank as he dug in his pocket for his phone, except for Carol, who saw an opportunity to escape. Running low, she shouldered past Jillian, dashed out of Louisa's room, and pounded down the stairs, crashing into the front door. She looked up just in time to see Ava grab the banister, jump onto the stairs, and then elegantly slip, resulting in her crashing and tumbling onto the landing and then sliding out the front door.

"Safe!" moaned Ava, hoping she was still alive.

"Get up!" shouted Carol, grabbing her by the shoulder and dragging her to her feet.

"I know," said Ava, dizzily shaking her head. "Run!"

14
THAT'S A LOT OF SQUARES

"I feel like the world's most-wanted fugitive," steamed Ava, collapsing onto her sofa. "All I ask is a chance to do my hair before they put my picture up on the most-wanted list."

"Worry about your hair later," chided Carol. She held up the metal cylinder that she found in the Alcott fireplace.

"I'll pretend you didn't say that," groaned Ava, climbing slowly to her feet.

"So, you really leaped over the railing onto the stairs?" asked Derik admiringly.

"Yep," nodded Ava. "And let me say, stair-surfing isn't as glamourous as it sounds. I heard crunching and cracking noises that I'd only expect from breakfast cereals."

"Snap, crackle, pop?" guessed Carol.

"Exactly," nodded Ava.

Carol turned the gray cylinder over in her hand, eyeing it closely like a jeweler. It was about the size of a ballpoint pen. The ends were sealed, and the outside was sticky and slick and covered in an oily ash. A thin line, like a piece of thread, circled around the middle.

"It probably twists open or just pulls apart," suggested Derik.

"That's what I figured," replied Carol, wiping the oily coating off with a napkin. She gripped each end of the tube and pulled. The cylinder smoothly separated into two parts. A tightly rolled piece of paper protruded from the half in her left hand.

"Awesome," whispered Ava, squeezing in closer between Carol and Derik for a closer look.

Carol carefully unrolled the paper onto the tabletop, holding the top and bottom with flat palms.

"What the heck?" asked Derik. "What is that?"

Carol shook her head. "I'm not sure." The paper was old and brittle; it had perhaps at one time been crisp and white, but now it was a sickly yellow color. It was also blank, but that wasn't the curious part. It was also riddled with dozens of rectangles that had been meticulously cut from the paper. It looked like an old computer punch card.

"It looks like what computers used to use before floppy disks or CDs," answered Carol. "But that doesn't make sense." She released the paper; it coiled back into a miniature scroll.

"None of this makes sense," replied Derik.

"Hold that thought," interrupted Ava, looking at her phone. "There's an email from Viva Renaissance, Incorporated." She opened the email and began to read,

Dearest Competitor,

Congratulations, my intrepid treasure hunters. My sources have informed me that several of you have solved a couple of the clues. Your success is to be commended.

My constituents and I have decided to raise the stakes of the contest. If you can find the location of the Crown Jewels within the next 24 hours, we will award you an additional $5,000. Cash! The clock is ticking!

Good luck and Godspeed!

Connor Bishop

CEO, Viva Renaissance, Incorporated

"Whoa. So, the reward is $15,000 now? That's a lot of money," said Carol.

"Too much money," said Derik, a confused look on his face. "Carol, may I use your laptop?"

"Sure." She spun her laptop around so it faced him.

"Okay," said Ava, leaning over his shoulder as he typed. "You wanna clue us in on your big secret?"

"Yeah." He paused for a second as he typed in the URL for Viva Renaissance, Incorporated. "I'm checking to see how many people signed up for the contest."

"Oh," said Ava, nodding. "Um, why?"

"Because," he pointed to the screen, "340 people registered."

"Yeah? So? He already said only a few people have been successful at figuring out the clues."

"Because," Carol answered for Derik, "the contest cost $50 to enter. If only 340 registered, that would equal $17,000."

"The reward is $15,000," explained Derik. "Not a very good business model if he is only making $2,000 for each contest. That would hardly cover his advertising cost."

"That's true," said Carol. "Placing that huge advertisement in the newspaper probably cost him several hundred dollars."

Ava gave Carol a worried look.

"I'm going to call Rebecca at my dad's bank," announced Derik. "She checks people's credit when they apply for a loan. I'll ask her to do a little background investigation on Viva Renaissance."

"Okay," exhaled Ava, calming herself. "Regardless of Connor Bishop's weird business habits, we've got to solve the clues before anyone else, or all of this is meaningless."

"Derik, make your call," said Carol. "Ava and I will try to solve the last clue."

"Perfect," smiled Derik. "And I'll try to figure out what this thing is," he offered, picking up the mysterious roll of paper from Carol's desk.

Ava picked up a dry erase marker and stepped back to read through the last clue silently in her head.

Ichabod's home, now a place of mortality. A circular stone, suggests punctuality. I depend on a star for the passage of time. Upon the hour of three, follow the line. The first chiseled words will reveal to you, the path that is just, the path that is true.

"All right, the clue's obviously about some dude named Ichabod." Ava wrote his name out on the crime board. "You know," she laughed, "his name sounds like what you would say if you found a dead body. *Ick, a bod!* Disgusting!"

"He did die by pumpkin," Carol reminded her.

"Oh, yeah. That's right. Didn't the Lone Ranger kill—"

"Headless Horseman," called out Derik, hanging up his phone. "The Headless Horseman chased down Ichabod Crane and *crowned* him with a pumpkin. See what I did there?"

"Nicely done," smiled Carol.

"I'm going to vomit," declared Ava. "Can we continue?"

"Fine," agreed Carol. "So, we know the clue is about Ichabod's home. If it's Ichabod Crane, then his home is Sleepy Hollow."

"Which is where?" asked Ava.

"Good question," replied Carol. "I'm not sure. Washington Irving wrote the short story, 'The Legend of Sleepy Hollow,' but I think the town, Sleepy Hollow, was made up."

"Great, we're looking for a fictional man in a fictional town." Ava wrote *Sleepy Hollow* on the board and put a question mark beside it.

"What about the next part?" prompted Ava.

"We've got a circular stone that suggests punctuality. He depends on a star for the passage of time," Carol mused.

"The sun is a star," called out Derik. "People used to use sundials to tell the time."

"It would make sense," said Carol excitedly. "A circular stone that suggests punctuality, and it uses the sun to tell time." She bent over her computer, and her fingers ran across the keyboard. "Look," she said, spinning her laptop around to face Ava.

Ava nodded. "Of course!" She stared at the circular slab of stone, a metal pole protruding from its center. Sequential numbers were carved around the perimeter. A thin black shadow extended from the base of the pole to the number five. "Five o' clock," whispered Ava, staring at the image on Carol's laptop. "So, it's basically saying, at three o'clock, we follow the line—or shadow—made by the sundial to the first chiseled clue."

"We're getting it," said Carol excitedly. "Let's put together what we know. First, we know that it's about Ichabod's home, which is Sleepy Hollow, but what gets me is the word *Now. Now a place of mortality.*"

Ava scratched her head and tapped the marker on the board. "What does mortality mean?"

"Death," replied Carol.

"*Ichabod's home,* now *a place of mortality,*" read Ava. "If Ichabod is dead, his home would be a graveyard. A place of mortality."

"Ava Clarke, you're brilliant!" exclaimed Carol.

"Of course, I am. Now, please tell me why."

"Sleepy Hollow Cemetery," said Carol excitedly, her fingers scrambling over her keyboard. "Ichabod's home was Sleepy Hollow. His home is now a graveyard: Sleepy Hollow Cemetery!"

"Awesome. How hard could it be to find a sundial in a cemetery?" asked Derik.

Carol pulled up the official website for Sleepy Hollow. "Um, says there are over ten thousand people buried there, and it's thirty-three acres."

"If we split up, we should be able to find it. It's almost eleven now. That gives us four hours before it's three o'clock," suggested Ava.

"Any luck over there, Derik?" asked Carol, stretching her arms to the ceiling.

"Well, I can tell you what it's not. It's not a computer punch card, and it's not an antique player piano music roll. Antique player pianos used to use rolls of paper with squares and rectangles punched out." He turned his laptop to show Ava and Carol.

"Wow," said Carol. "It actually looks really similar."

"Yeah. I'll figure it out," he said, closing the top of his laptop. "I texted a picture to my dad to see if he had any ideas, but he's in a meeting right now."

"We're so close," said Ava. "I can feel it in my bones!"

"That feeling in your bones…it's probably from you falling down the stairs," winked Derik.

15
SLEEPY HOLLOW CEMETERY

"Why do they put fences around cemeteries?" asked Ava gravely. "Because people are dying to get in."

"She's your best friend," said Derik to Carol, eyes filled with pity.

To say that Sleepy Hollow Cemetery was massive would have been a gross understatement. Row after row of gravestones of all shapes, colors, and sizes erupted from the earth like teeth. Several roads snaked around grassy knolls filled with grave markers, family burial plots, and obelisks. The trio watched a young boy on a skateboard whiz by.

"Well," commented Ava, "that's not something you see every day."

"Isn't Louisa May Alcott buried here?" asked Derik.

"Yes, most of her family is buried here on Author's Ridge. The website also said that Ralph Waldo Emerson, Nathaniel Hawthorne, and Henry David Thoreau are buried here as well." Carol explained.

"It's really incredible," said Derik thoughtfully. "So many famous people."

"Where do we start?" asked Ava. "It's overwhelming."

"Ava, why don't you take Author's Gate? I'll take the Wood Gate area, and Derik, you hit the New Hill Gate. Start at the outside and work your way in toward the center."

"Got it," said Ava, pedaling off. Seconds later, she circled back. "Just curious—where is Author's Gate?"

***

Carol found the cemetery to be both fascinating and tragic. Each gravestone told a story, some in words, some in pictures. She stopped in front of a simple tiny grave. The inscription read, *Our darling Lucy, June 6, 1872—December 23, 1885.*

She was the same age as me, thought Carol. *And two days before Christmas.* She reached down and gathered a handful of wildflowers and lay them in front of the gravestone. *Rest in peace, Lucy.*

Derik texted Ava and Carol with a progress report—he'd spent the past hour searching for anything that resembled a sundial. So far, nothing.

Ava hadn't had any luck either. She had found the Alcott family's burial site. She was struck by the size and plainness of Louisa's tombstone. It was a simple arched piece of stone with the letters *L.M.A.* carved into it, and the dates *1832—1888* carved below it. *So ordinarily simple,* thought Ava. So unlike the grandeur Ava felt she deserved.

Carol's stomach growled. She glanced at her watch. It was nearly two o'clock, and they were running out of time. She pulled out her phone and began Googling to see if there was a famous sundial in the cemetery. She scrolled through page after page but found nothing.

Suddenly, her phone buzzed. "Ava," she whispered softly, "tell me you found something." She opened the text and exhaled. It was a selfie of Ava, and behind her, a sundial the size of a truck tire. "Thank God!"

Where are you? Carol texted.

Crescent Avenue, Ava responded. *Derik's on his way.*

Derik dropped his bike to the ground and ran to join Ava and Carol, who were standing in front of a large sundial atop a small, grassy hill.

"Dude," exclaimed Derik, eyeing the sundial. "That thing is awesome—and almost right on time," he noted, looking at his phone.

"So," said Carol, bringing their attention back to the matter at hand, "the clue said, *Upon the hour of three, follow the line. The first chiseled words will reveal to you, the path that is just, the path that is true.*"

"If we're simply following a line created by the sun, we really don't need to wait until three o'clock. We can pretty much guestimate," suggested Ava.

"Yep," said Carol, aligning herself with the number 3 on the sundial. "If I walk like I'm on a tightrope…," she stepped, placing one foot in front of the other, "…it takes me here." She stopped in front of a rectangular, granite gravestone hidden behind a forest of weeds.

Carol knelt and pulled away the weeds; the fresh smell of dirt and grass filled her nose. She wiped her nose with her sleeve, holding back a sneeze.

"What does it say?" asked Ava.

"Safe at home, in God's hands," Carol read.

There was no name or date—simply the number 42 carved into the stone below the phrase.

"The first chiseled words will reveal to you, the path that is just, the path that is true," uttered Carol. *"Safe at home,"* she whispered, thinking.

"Safe at home," repeated Ava.

Carol looked at Ava and Derik, tilting her head. "You don't think that it's that simple, do you?"

Derik was about to reply when his phone rang. He held up a finger, spoke for a minute, and then hung up the phone.

"That was my dad. No offense," he said, "but my dad was surprised that you two didn't know what the paper was."

"I have my theories," said Ava. "I just prefer to keep them to myself until someone else discovers them for me."

Derik shook his head, not sure how to respond. "I'm just gonna finish up with what my dad told me. He said the piece of paper is most likely a cipher key."

"A cipher key," said Carol excitedly. "How does it work?"

"Let's say that I'm a spy, and I've agreed to leave hidden messages for you at a certain library. I wouldn't want to leave the actual message there, for fear of someone finding it and figuring it out. Instead, we could agree on a very obscure book to pass secret messages to each other. I could simply say, page 72. You would take the cipher card with the punched-out holes and place it over page 72. The letters that are revealed are my secret code."

"Oh, cool," exclaimed Ava. "So, we could just keep using the same page—"

"And use a new cipher paper each time. You just cut out new squares each time to deliver a different message."

"That's brilliantly cool," declared Ava.

"Only," added Carol, "like Derik mentioned, you have to know the source used as the key. We have no idea what he used as the key. It could be anything."

"Well," said Ava, thinking aloud. "It's unlikely they would include something in the contest that we wouldn't have access to."

"She's right," nodded Derik. "And just like Ava, I have a theory."

"Oh, well, sharing is caring," said Carol.

"Let's get back to The Lair," said Derik. "I'll show you there."

"Oh, you're gonna keep us in suspense. I think Jillian must be rubbing off on him," said Ava, narrowing her eyes.

"Will Derik solve the mystery of the enigmatic paper? Stay tuned to find out!" Derik said theatrically.

"Oh, brother," moaned Carol, pulling the hood of his hoodie over his head.

16
THE CIPHER

Derik made a beeline for the crime board, grabbing a piece of paper attached by a magnet. "Remember when you printed this?" he asked, waving the piece of paper in his hand. "You said it looked fancy."

"Yeah, it looked like an old-fashioned, handwritten letter," Carol said.

"Exactly, like someone had written the clues a long time ago. If I'm right…," he placed the paper on Carol's desk and grabbed the coiled cipher paper, "…then the places that were cut out should align with letters on this handwritten paper."

Derik carefully smoothed out the rolled cipher key over the letters, aligning it with the text on the page.

"It's working," whispered Carol. "I see letters in all the squares." She raced over to the crime board and grabbed a dry erase marker. "Call out the letters!"

"Okay." Derik closed one eye and leaned in. "O-N-E-T-W-O-O-N-E-B-I-R-C-H-S-T-C-O-N-C-O-R-D-M-A."

"One, two, one, Birch St," said Carol excitedly.

"Birch Street," exclaimed Ava. "It's Birch Street."

"In Concord, Massachusetts," finished off Derik.

Ava flipped open her laptop and typed *121 Birch Street, Concord, MA* into Google. "It's a bed and breakfast called

Gallagher's Inn. Hmm." Ava continued reading aloud. "*It was built in 1811 and purchased by Patrick Gallagher when he moved here from Ireland in 1907, when he turned the home into a bed and breakfast.*"

Carol looked at Derik. "Weren't Ireland's Crown Jewels stolen in 1907? You don't think these are the real Crown Jewels, do you?"

Derik made a face and nodded. "I'm almost positive."

"You guys are forgetting something: We've solved all of the clues, but even if we find a safe, we can't get inside it."

"I can't imagine that they would give us the clues and then not give us the combination," said Derik.

"Maybe he did give us the combination," said Carol, pointing to the crime board. "Remember, all but one of the clues included a number, and we could never figure out why: 38, 17, and 42."

"How much do you want to bet that those three numbers open the safe?" asked Ava excitedly.

"Only one way to find out," said Carol, grabbing her backpack and flinging it over her shoulder.

"Wait," said Ava, looking as if she were going to be sick. "I hate, yet again, to be the voice of reason, but we can't just walk into someone's home and start poking around." She switched to a theatric tone. "Hi, Mr. Gallagher, we're here to rummage through your house and perhaps break into your safe, if you don't mind!"

"True," agreed Carol, "however, your story is flawed. Mr. Gallagher bought the house in 1907. In your scenario, Mr. Gallagher would have to be around 150 years old."

"Maybe he did yoga and only ate organic fruits and vegetables," Ava countered.

"Or," added Derik, "he drank from the fountain of youth. Don't laugh. Some people say that George Clooney is actually Ponce de León. Google it—their likeness is uncanny."

"Uncanny?" asked Ava.

"Yes," replied Carol, "unlikely to be canned."

"Okay," said Ava, reading further down the Gallagher Inn web page. "It looks like the house is now owned by Mildred Gallagher, Patrick's great-granddaughter. This is getting weirder and weirder."

Derik nodded. "Let's see if there is a safe, and if this combination works. I gotta tell you, though, something doesn't feel right. I mean, I may be wrong, maybe this is truly a contest, and this Bishop guy just loves doing these contests and isn't in it for the money."

The look on Ava's and Carol's face told him they were thinking the same thing.

"But," he continued, "I think there's another mystery buried beneath all of this."

"I do too," agreed Carol, "but for now, let's proceed one step at a time, and currently, our biggest problem is finding and getting to the safe."

"I've been thinking…," Ava began.

"Well, there's a first for everything," interjected Carol.

"I say," continued Ava, "we take a page from Derik's brilliant playbook and keep it simple."

"Did you hear that?" smiled Derik, nudging Carol. "She said I'm brilliant."

"Not you," clarified Ava. "Your playbook."

"Brilliant by association," sighed Derik. He fluttered his hands at Ava. "Go ahead and finish with your speech."

"Thank you. The plan is simple. I turn on Facetime. I knock on her door. When Mildred answers, I'll give her a woeful story about my school report that I'm writing and that I found her historical bed and breakfast online, and, well, I just *have* to write my report about this house and her great-grandfather, Patrick."

"Go on," said Derik, waving his hand.

"Once I get her away from the door and into another room, I'll say something that won't raise suspicion, like *rutabaga*."

"How about, *The raven crows at midnight?*" suggested Derik.

"The code word needs to fit into the situation," Carol said. "Tell her you find the interior of the house stunning. The code word is *stunning*. Can you remember that?"

"Sure," nodded Ava. "It's literally the first thing that comes to mind when I see myself in the mirror."

"Hmm," said Carol, smirking. "I thought it'd be vapid."

17
GALLAGHER'S INN

"Mrs. Gallagher?" asked Ava, stretching out her hand. Ava needn't have asked—she immediately recognized the woman from the inn's website. Short white hair chopped unevenly halfway down her ears. Pale-blue, intelligent eyes that stared back at Ava behind ruby-red framed glasses.

"Yes," answered the woman, grasping Ava's hand. "Do I know you?"

"I'm Ava Clarke, and I love your dress," she gushed, admiring Mildred's pale-blue dress adorned with creamy white flowers.

"Thank you, Miss Clarke," she said, tilting her head in appreciation. "How can I help you?"

"May I come in?" asked Ava, giving Mildred her biggest smile. "I assure you, my visit is educationally motivated."

"Um, certainly," said Mildred, still somewhat puzzled by Ava's presence.

"Please let me explain and apologize for such an abrupt visit. I attend Noble Park Middle School, and I'm in the gifted program."

Ava paused for a second, expecting to hear a snicker from the bushes where Carol and Derik were hiding, but thankfully, the only sound was the air filter in Mrs. Gallagher's hallway.

"We've been assigned the task of researching places of historical significance. Most of my classmates of course jumped on the usuals: the Orchard House, the Hawthorne Inn…. I wanted to tell the story of an immigrant coming from Ireland with a dream."

"I see," said Mrs. Gallagher softly.

"Is that Patrick Gallagher?" asked Ava, gesturing toward a painting that hung at the base of a winding stairway.

"Yes," said Mrs. Gallagher, turning. "That's a picture of my great-grandfather." She seemed pleased that Ava recognized the picture.

"He's so regal," said Ava, fighting desperately to find the right word. "I know you are probably incredibly busy, running such an exquisite estate, but could you please spare a few minutes to show me around?"

Mrs. Gallagher glanced at a delicate silver watch and then smiled. "Why not?"

Ava smiled back, swallowing the lump of anxiety lodged in her throat like a piece of hard candy that threatened to choke her.

"Let's start with the kitchen," chirped Mrs. Gallagher. "It's my guests' favorite room."

"Wonderful," gushed Ava as she followed her down the hallway leading to the kitchen. Ava stopped and pointed to an intricate piece of needlepoint framed on the wall.

"Ah, that piece," smiled Mrs. Gallagher. "You know, you walk through this house and you forget to take in the simple things. My grandmother made that for me. It's the family's seal. She gave it to me when I was seven years old."

"The needlework is so complex," said Ava, shaking her head.

"All done by hand—not like nowadays, where you push a button and a machine does everything. That piece of needlepoint took Granny eight months to create."

"It's stunning," said Ava as they walked toward the kitchen. "Absolutely stunning."

"That's our code word," whispered Carol. She peeked around the flowing juniper shrub she and Derik were hidden behind. "Coast is clear. Let's go."

"Everything about this house is blue," said Derik quietly as they tiptoed up the blue-and-white wooden porch steps.

Carol held her finger to her lips and slowly opened the blue door, which opened into a small foyer. The house was set up like a lowercase *t*. A hallway and set of stairs appeared to the left, and another short hallway that led to the living room was on the right. Directly in front of them was a narrow hallway that led to the back of the house.

Carol could clearly hear Ava's animated voice from the left side of the house. She motioned for Derik to go to the room on the right. If Derik thought the outside of the house was blue, he hadn't seen anything yet. The living room looked as if someone had attached a sprinkler to a can of blue paint and let it rip.

The walls were a beautiful cornflower-blue and adorned with pale white daisies. A blue sofa with golden pillows sat against a wall, and at the end of the room stood a blue fireplace with a blue mantel. The only thing in the room that wasn't blue was a wooden table that sat across the room from the sofa. By the table was a wrought iron chair with a golden seat cushion.

"I don't think the safe would be in here. It's most likely in their home office or study," said Derik.

Carol nodded, kicking herself for not looking up the floorplan to the house before they arrived. "Let's see where that door leads," she said, pointing to a door at the end of the room, adjacent to the fireplace. Carol gently eased the door open. "Bingo," she whispered.

"You found something?" Derik asked.

"No," said Carol, shaking her head. "It's a game closet. See? Bingo."

Derik stuck his head in the doorway. Sure enough, it was a closet filled with puzzles and games. "Probably for the guests," suggested Derik.

Carol and Derik backtracked to the foyer and took the hallway leading to the back of the house. The first door they came to opened into a closet filled with winter clothes, and the second door was locked.

Derik leaned in and whispered, "I bet it's the office."

Carol nodded, pulling out her library card. "I know," she muttered, seeing the dismayed look on Derik's face. "Blame it on Ava. She's a bad influence."

Moments later, they were in another blue room.

"If there's ever a world shortage on blue paint," whispered Derik, "we know where it all went."

Carol slowly turned, taking in the room. Each side was filled with wall-to-wall bookshelves. In the center of the room was a beautiful wooden desk, facing a window that looked out onto a forest filled with oak, maple, and pine trees. The surface of the desk was empty, except for a laptop and two sets of pictures that Carol assumed were of her grandchildren.

Only one wall was empty, save for a striking piece of artwork. Two incredibly detailed hands, worn and rough, were pressed together as if in prayer. Shards of golden light radiated from around the hands, diffusing into the blackest of black backgrounds.

Derik gently pulled the ornate painting from the wall and smiled. They'd found the safe. "Grab the other side of the painting," whispered Derik.

Just as Carol's fingers encircled around the frame, the doorbell rang. She looked at Derik. "Hide!"

***

"One moment, dear," said Mrs. Gallagher to Ava. "Someone's at the door. Probably the post or UPS."

"No worries. I'm truly enjoying myself," said Ava, following her from the kitchen to the foyer.

Ava's jaw dropped when Mildred opened the front door. Even though she was wearing a wig and sunglasses, Ava recognized Jillian—and her producer, who was wearing the most pitiful excuse for a fake mustache she'd ever seen.

Jillian delicately removed her sunglasses and placed them in her Prada handbag. Her eyes lowered and met Ava's for a second and then flashed upward to Mrs. Gallagher, a huge smile crossing her face.

Ava decided to immediately go on the offensive. "Fancy meeting you here," gushed Ava, stepping in between Mrs. Gallagher, Jillian, and Frank.

"You two know each other?" asked Mrs. Gallagher, surprised.

"Yes," said Ava before Jillian could respond. "Mrs. Gallagher, this is Karen and Wilbur Wright. She's my mom's water aerobics instructor. My mom says she is truly gifted and that her choreography is inspiring, and Wilbur is a professional whittler. He's writing a screenplay about his creations—I believe it's called *Whittler on the Roof*?" asked Ava innocently.

"Such a marvelous and precocious child," said Jillian, tweaking Ava's cheeks. "My husband and I were having lunch at the Colonial Inn, and we were discussing having some friends come stay here in October. And, since we were right down the street, we were wondering if we could maybe take a look at your accommodations and any information you may have available."

Nicely done, thought Ava.

"Yes," Mrs. Gallagher began.

"Mildred," came a raspy voice at the top of the stairs. "I have an important meeting, and I can't seem to get a wireless connection on my laptop."

"I'll be right there, Mr. Mathers," she called up before bringing her attention back to her newest guests. "Please come in," said Mrs. Gallagher, motioning to Jillian and her producer. "The living room is right over there," she continued, gesturing to her left. "You'll find some pamphlets and brochures there. Please make yourself at home."

"Thank you," smiled Jillian, brandishing her toothy, trademark smile. She waited until Mrs. Gallagher had disappeared and then turned to face Ava, the smile melting away from her face. "All right," she snarled. "Where are they?"

"Who?" asked Ava innocently.

"Are we really going to play this game?" hissed Jillian. "We followed you here. Either you come clean or Mrs. Gallagher is going to find out your little scheme."

Ava felt the tips of her ears burning. She liked Mrs. Gallagher and hated the thought of having to lie to her, but....

Ava tried to reason with herself. Maybe Mrs. Gallagher was in on the contest. She would have to be, right? The safe was in her house, and all the clues led them here.

"Well," snapped Jillian. "What's it going to be?"

Ava reached into her pocket and pulled out her phone. "Where are you?" she whispered.

"In the study," replied Carol angrily. "We heard everything. Take the hall parallel to the stairway, second door on the right."

***

Derik and Carol quickly removed the picture from the wall and rested it on the floor against a chair, just as Ava, Jillian, and Frank walked in the door.

"The safe's already open," said Jillian suspiciously. "See? It's not closed all the way."

"What?" asked Carol, bewildered. Sure enough, the door to the safe wasn't latched. She swung the door of the safe open. "Someone's beaten us here! It's...it's empty," she gasped.

"Liars," spat Jillian angrily. "Where are the jewels? Where did you hide them?"

"Wait," exclaimed Derik. "Everyone calm down. I have seen safes like this."

Jillian and Frank looked at him curiously.

"My family's been in banking for the past two hundred years. This safe most likely has a second panel that's hidden."

Jillian hesitated and looked at Derik shrewdly. "If you knew there was a hidden compartment, why did you tell us? Why not just sneak back and get the jewels later?"

"Why is this so important to you? Ratings? Another year-long contract for *Expedition Miraculous*?" hissed Carol.

"I could ask you the same question," sneered Jillian. "Why is it so important to you?"

"People like you wouldn't care. You're heartless," Carol snarled.

"Carol," said Ava, putting a comforting hand on her friend's shoulder. "We need the money to help a friend of ours. Her daughter, London, is deaf, and the money from the contest...," Ava sucked in her breath, "...was to pay for a life-changing surgery so she can hear again."

Jillian looked from Derik to Ava to Carol, as if waiting for the punchline to a joke. Jillian's face dropped. "You three have gone through all of this to help a friend's daughter?"

"She's a single mom," said Carol, "just trying to give her daughter an amazing gift."

"Guys," said Derik. "There's a lot of emotion in the room right now. Can I make a suggestion that is a win-win for everyone?"

"You've got our attention," said Ava.

The others nodded silently.

"Jillian, you're filming an episode for *Expedition Miraculous*. We don't care about the glory of finding the jewels. We simply need the reward money for London. Why don't we film you opening the safe and finding the jewels? We'll take the Crown Jewels to Mr. Bishop, and we'll split the reward money with you fifty-fifty. Do we have a deal?"

Jillian looked at Frank, who in turn gave her an *Are you kidding me? Take the deal!* look.

"Wait," said Ava. "Then we won't have enough for the surgery."

"We'll find a way," said Derik firmly. "But right now, time isn't on our side. We've got to make a deal."

"I guess we have no other choice," whispered Ava angrily.

"Okay," nodded Jillian. "We'll take the deal."

"Of course, you will," mumbled Carol bitterly.

Derik closed the safe and twisted the combination dial. "The safe works just like your typical combination lock," he explained. "Twist clockwise to the first number, counterclockwise to the second number, and then clockwise to the third number."

"Got it," said Jillian. "What's the combination?"

"Thirty-eight." He waited as she turned the dial. "Seventeen. Forty-two." There was a soft click, and then the door swung open. Frank moved in, zooming in on the interior of the safe.

"The jewels," gushed Jillian. "We've found the jewels." Laying on a piece of black felt was the Grand Master's diamond star, along with the Collar Badge of Knight Companion, and the Grand Master's diamond badge.

The words had barely escaped her lips when they heard footsteps coming down the stairs. Derik shot his hand inside the safe, grabbing the jewels. "Meet us at Dillard's Donut Shack in thirty minutes!" he yelled.

Carol raced to the window and threw it open. Carol and Derik jumped out, leaving Jillian, Frank, and Ava to deal with Mrs. Gallagher.

18
THE CHASE

Carol's phone buzzed. "They'll be here in two minutes," she said, looking at Derik.

"Okay." He nodded. "I talked to my dad. Everything's in place."

"I'm conflicted," said Carol sadly. "It's amazing news, and it's sad news at the same time."

"I know," said Derik. "Don't worry," he encouraged. "We'll figure something out."

"They're here," nodded Carol, as a black van pulled up to the curb.

"This *so* looks like the beginning of a stranger-danger video," complained Derik as he approached the van.

"Agreed," sighed Carol, sliding open the side door.

***

"Are you sure they're real?" asked Jillian, trembling with excitement. She'd climbed into the back of the van to sit with Ava, Carol, and Derik.

"Yes," nodded Derik. "Mr. Nakamura is a mega-well-respected jeweler, with clientele from all over the world. My dad has been working with him for nearly twenty years. If he says the jewels are real, then they're real."

Jillian fell back against her seat. "This is better than I ever imagined. We never actually find anything on *Expedition Miraculous*. I hype each show with some huge discovery, but in the end, we never actually discovered anything."

"I'm happy for you," said Carol quietly. "I hope that this helps to keep your show on the air."

"Thank you," said Jillian. "I'm sorry that I was such a jerk. It's a hyper-competitive world out there. You gotta—"

"We're here," Frank interrupted, pulling the van up to a two-story, red-brick building. "Looks like Mr. Bishop's office is on the second floor."

Derik handed Jillian a black cloth bag, cinched together and tied into a loose knot at the top. "You do the honors."

"They said no cameras allowed," stated Ava. "How is Frank supposed to film?"

Frank turned in his seat and smiled, tapping his thick-framed black glasses. "Do you see that tiny, tiny, hole on the nose piece?"

"No," answered Ava, leaning forward in her seat. Carol and Derik also shook their heads.

"Good," laughed Frank. "There's a tiny video camera in my glasses. Don't worry. this isn't my first rodeo."

"Hmm," smiled Carol. "Derik, perhaps after this is all over, you and Frank should hang out. You can tell him how you lassoed a statue."

"Maybe so," winked Frank.

***

The front door opened to a narrow set of stairs covered in gray carpeting. The walls were eggshell white and smelled like they were freshly painted. Jillian and Frank clomped ahead. The group stopped, staggered on the stairway, looking as if they were about to storm a castle. A glass door with the words *Viva Renaissance, Inc.* was all that stood between them and victory.

"He should have had whoever built his website do the lettering for his door," said Carol, pointing out that the words *Viva Renaissance, Inc.* were obviously made by a store-bought self-stencil kit.

"No kidding," whispered Ava. "Nothing says authority like do-it-yourself stencils."

Jillian snickered and looked back over her shoulder at Ava and Carol. "Are you two always like this?"

"As an outside observer," offered Derik, "I would say that is a resounding yes."

"Okay, everyone," said Frank quietly, touching a button by the hinge of his glasses. "We're rolling!"

Jillian pushed the door, holding it open for Frank so he could get into the optimum position to film all the action with his secret camera glasses. Ava, Carol, and Derik quickly filed in behind him, careful to stay out of his shot.

The room was small. There was a tiny two-person couch, a small window facing the street, two paintings of large mallards that looked like they came from Pier One's discount rack, and a tall black lamp that resembled a hydra. At the back of the room, a woman sat behind a large, solid rectangular desk…or barrier.

The woman stood and clapped her hands excitedly as everyone entered the room. She crinkled her tiny nose and shook her body back and forth like a bowling pin about to topple over.

Ava narrowed her eyes, trying to figure out what was going on with the woman's hair. It was reddish brown with blond highlights. On one side of her head it was bunched up like a bun, while on the other side, it was flowy and wavy across her shoulder. It looked like a fox was napping on top of her head.

She wore a simple gray sweater with a white collar and white stretch pants secured with a silver belt and silver buckle. Her eyes were a beautiful aqua color. Ava was pretty sure that was due to colored contacts.

"Hello," the woman chirped. "I'm Genie." Her voice was high and excited.

"Hello," replied Jillian. "We're here to claim the prize for the contest!" She raised the cloth bag as she spoke. "We've found the Crown Jewels."

"You found them? You really found them?" the woman gushed.

Jillian rested the cloth bag on her leg, untied the string, and removed the Grand Master's diamond badge. The jewelry sparkled brilliantly in her hand.

"Incredible," the woman whispered, her eyes as big as saucers. "Just one moment," she said, holding up a finger. "Mr. Bishop is going to want to personally give you the reward. You must be so excited." She cradled her phone against her ear with her shoulder.

Jillian didn't speak; she merely smiled at the woman, waiting for her to finish her call.

"Yes, sir," said Genie. "Yes, they have brought the jewels with them." She paused for a moment and looked at Jillian. "She showed me the Grand Master's diamond badge," she said into the phone. Genie looked up and gave them an *I'm sorry this is taking so long* look.

The group as a whole smiled back at her. "We understand," whispered Jillian.

"Mr. Bishop would like to take a moment to personally inspect the jewels," Genie declared, hanging up the phone. "He's had, well, he's had issues before with competitors."

The group looked at each other warily, but Jillian acquiesced and offered the woman the cloth bag. "This won't take long, will it?" asked Jillian. "I have a flight to catch."

"Merely two minutes," she replied, taking the bag from Jillian and clutching it to her chest. Genie turned and opened a white door directly behind her desk. "Just one teeny moment." She smiled as she closed the door behind her.

"So, what do you think's going to happen?" asked Frank.

Jillian shrugged. "Either they give us a check and it's fake, or...."

"Or they take off running out the back door," said Derik, pointing out the window.

"Come on!" yelled Ava, racing down the steps to the front door. Ava, Carol, and Derik burst out onto the sidewalk, followed by Jillian and Frank.

Chirp, chirp.

Carol whipped her head around, following the telltale noise of a car fob being activated. Genie and Connor Bishop were sliding into a black BMW. "There!" yelled Carol, jabbing her finger at the car.

"Oh, no, you don't!" screamed Ava, sprinting off down the sidewalk.

"What's she going to do?" yelled Jillian in stunned disbelief.

"Something crazy," Carol hollered back knowingly. "Something crazy."

Connor's car was squeezed in between two other cars, but he didn't seem to mind. He gunned his engine, slamming the back of his car into a red Mini Cooper, pushing it backward. The BMW's tires squealed, sending up a cloud of smoke.

That's when Ava launched herself on top of his car and spread out over his front window like a beautiful starfish with purple highlights.

Connor blasted his horn. The sound was so loud it made Ava's eyes go cross, but like an enraged suckerfish she held her position on the front window. Genie reached over and twisted the switch for the windshield wipers, which began to smack Ava in the face over and over again. *Screech-smack, screech-smack.*

Connor leaned out his window and shook his fist at her. "Get off my car, or I'm going to crush you!"

"Hah!" yelled Ava. "You wouldn't dare! Your insurance will go up!"

Just then, Genie found the windshield washer button and sprayed Ava in the face with soapy water.

"Argh," screamed Ava, taking jets of cold water to her face. "You animal!"

"I warned you to get off my car," screamed Connor, revving his engine and throwing his car in reverse. "Now, I'm going to make you!"

Carol watched in horror as Connor shot forward, slamming his car into the blue Ford Mustang in front of him. The Mustang's car alarm began whooping angrily.

Ava clung to the top of the car, her body flying to the side, her fingers fighting to keep their grip.

Connor gunned his engine and was about to slam into the Mini Cooper again when he was hauled out of his seat and yanked through his car window. Ava turned her head and smiled at a police officer who looked like a bulldozer with a buzz cut. The bulldozer cop was holding Connor Bishop in the air with one arm.

"Officer Tiny," whispered Ava, dropping her head to the windshield. "You made it."

Officer Tiny smiled a huge toothy grin at her as he pushed Connor against the car, snapping handcuffs around his wrist. "I didn't want to interrupt your ride," he laughed.

"Ava, you okay?" asked a gruff voice. She raised her head and looked to the left. "Detective Edwards," she smiled. "You always look like you stepped out of a fashion magazine. You're my inspiration."

Detective Edwards shook his head, dark brown eyes filled with concern and pride. "Ava Clarke, did you think you could wrestle a car?"

"No," she laughed, climbing down off the hood, wiping her face with her arm. "But I bet Tiny could."

Officer Tiny came over and gave her a hug. "Great job, kid, on catching these two clowns."

"I had a lot of help," smiled Ava, looking at her friends as they gathered around.

"You're the woman from *Expedition Miraculous*," stammered Officer Tiny.

"Yes. Yes, I am. I'm Jillian Steele, and you are...?"

"A fan. Your biggest fan!"

"Well," said Carol, leaning onto her friend's shoulder. "He's not lying. He is probably her biggest fan."

"I love your show," Tiny stammered on. "I watch it every week. My favorite was when you were in the castle in Transylvania. No. No, when you were in Egypt—"

"Oh," gushed Jillian. "Being in Romania was one of the most exciting adventures I've ever been on."

"And...I think we've lost them," laughed Carol.

Detective Edwards looked at Officer Tiny gushing all over Jillian and shook his head. "Okay," he sighed. "So, who's this?" He looked at the woman in the car.

"She said her name is Genie," answered Carol. "We know that's probably not true, but we do know she is Connor's crony."

Genie sat unmoving and staring out the front window, clutching the Crown Jewels to her chest.

"And Ireland's Crown Jewels are in the bag she's squeezing to her chest like a teddy bear," Carol continued.

"The Crown Jewels of Ireland?" asked Detective Edwards. He shook his head and opened the door. "Step out, please, ma'am."

Carol wasn't sure what it was that tipped her off—a tightening of the jaw, a miniscule dropping of the shoulders. But something told her that Genie was going to run, and run she did.

Genie had kicked off her shoes, and when the door opened, she bolted—right past Jillian and Officer Tiny, who were deep in conversation about *Expedition Miraculous*—down the sidewalk in her mismatched socks.

For the second time in a matter of minutes, Carol and Ava were wildly dashing after a criminal. Carol put on a burst of speed, quickly closing the gap.

Genie, obviously a novice escapee, made the rookie mistake of looking over her shoulder at her pursuer as she fled and slammed into an open car door as a result. To her credit—and Carol's surprise—she leapt to her feet, wobbled, shook her head, and took off running again.

"Stop!" screamed Carol, her black Converse sneakers skidding to a halt.

But Genie didn't stop, and like a one-woman running of the bulls, she continued, crashing through a construction barricade and entangling herself in a web of yellow tape and cones. She then disappeared, like a whack-a-mole, into a manhole.

"You okay?" yelled Carol, hovering over the manhole opening on her hands and knees.

Moments later, the most pitiful, faint "Ouch" emerged from the darkness, reminding Carol of one of her favorite movies: *Horton Hears a Who*.

19
FORGIVENESS

"I talked to my dad," said Derik, plopping down on the sofa between Ava and Carol. "He said if we start a GoFundMe page for Kaitlyn and London, the bank will donate a thousand dollars."

"Whoa, that's so incredibly cool of your dad," said Ava excitedly.

"He also said that he bets that a lot of the local businesses would also donate."

"I love the idea," said Carol. "I really do, but we have to be careful."

"What do you mean?" asked Derik.

"We don't want to do anything to embarrass Kaitlyn. She'll be upset if it feels too much like charity."

"Yeah, but we told her if we won the competition that we would give her part of it, and we did solve the mystery," pointed out Ava.

"You know what I mean," said Carol. "Everyone here knows that it was a big scam. It was front page in the newspaper and on the news last night. I'm sure Kaitlyn knows what happened. I really want to help…," Carol began, but was cut off by Ava's mom peeking her head into the doorway of The Lair.

"There's someone here to see you," she chirped excitedly, as a familiar pair entered.

"Jillian!" said Ava, jumping to her feet. "Frank! What are you doing here? We thought you would be back in Hollywood, or wherever it is you live while getting ready for the premiere of your show!"

"Well, we were in the neighborhood," Jillian began.

"She has a dinner date with Officer Tiny," Frank winked.

Jillian smacked him on the back of the head. "We're just friends," she clarified. "Ahem," she continued. "As I was saying before I was rudely interrupted, we were in the neighborhood, and we thought we'd stop by." She turned in a slow circle, taking in The Lair. "So, this is where all of the investigative magic happens?"

"Yes," smiled Ava proudly. "We call it The Lair."

"The Lair," said Frank. "I love it! Cool drone, by the way. I used one of those just recently. Hopefully you'll see it on tonight's show."

"Congratulations on having your series renewed. I hear the Crown Jewels episode is going to run tonight," said Carol.

"Thank you," said Jillian kindly. "It's a huge deal. Actually, that's why I'm here." She smiled mischievously. "I told my friends at the network about you guys and how you made so many sacrifices for your friend." She shook her head, and her face softened. "You reminded me of who I used to be. Tenacious. Unbending. I was a force to be reckoned with. But slowly and surely, I began to change. Soon, it was no longer about the story or the adventure. Instead, it was about how many people liked my Instagram post. How were my ratings? How could I promote myself?"

She looked at Frank and gave him an affectionate smile. "I lost touch of my good qualities. My curiosity and thirst for adventure. My friendships. Watching you three risking everything simply to make life better for someone else, well...," she caught her breath, "...was inspiring."

She bit her lip and wiped the back of her hand across her eyes. She smiled broadly. "So, the network and I would like to give you a little gift for London." Jillian looked at Carol in the eye and revealed an envelope. "This is for your friend."

Carol took the envelope from her, her hands trembling so badly she could barely open it. Tears spilled down Carol's face. "It's...it's a check for twenty thousand dollars," she stuttered.

She looked at Ava and Derik and then ran toward Jillian, throwing her arms around her waist. "Thank you, Jillian, Thank you."

***

Ava, Derik, and Carol sat on the sofa in The Lair. Ava settled in the middle, a humongous bowl of popcorn balanced on her lap. Carol grabbed the television remote and navigated to Channel 17.

A tidal wave of music filled the room, a streak of fire burned across the screen, and then the golden background exploded into tiny fiery pieces that came back together to spell *Expedition Miraculous*.

It was fun to watch Jillian work through the clues and see how she tied the story together; she was a natural storyteller. Carol appreciated the fact that she mixed in a lot of historical elements into the show.

"Well," said Ava, as the show returned from a commercial break, "here comes the big reveal."

The show started with a quick recap, and then there they were, at the safe. The trio sat quietly, feeling a bit betrayed as they watched Jillian open the safe. The blasting music crescendoed as the camera zoomed in, revealing the Crown Jewels.

"Well," said Carol. "I guess we both got…."

Carol stopped talking and stared at the television. A smiling Jillian in a black T-shirt and black jeans filled the screen; a bright piano melody played in the background. "It would be easy to take credit for solving all of the clues and finding the Crown Jewels, but the truth is, I couldn't have done it all by myself." She smiled and stepped off camera.

Suddenly, video of Derik repelling down the church steeple appeared.

"That's me," said Derik, hopping up from the couch and knocking the bowl of popcorn out of Ava's lap.

"Heeeey," Ava cried as her snack fell.

"That's me!" Derik repeated.

The next video showed the three friends in the graveyard, and then Ava diving onto Connor Bishop's car, being flung back and forth like a ragdoll. That was followed by Carol racing down the sidewalk after Genie, ending with her disappearing down the manhole.

It was the last piece of video that brought smiles to all three friends. Somehow, Frank had captured video of Ava, Carol, and Derik walking down the sidewalk together side by side.

Jillian left the image of the three friends standing together as she positioned herself once more in front of the camera.

"None of this would have been possible without my new incredible friends. Ava Clarke, Carol Miller, and Derik Charter. These three very special people are the true heroes of the story. They reminded me that there is something more valuable than fame, more valuable than jewels, and that is true friendship." Jillian smiled and raised her hands to her chest, forming them into the shape of a heart. "Thank you."

20
NOW I GET IT

"Well," said Derik, rolling his bike into the bike rack at the Dillard's Donut Shack, "did you talk to Detective Edwards as to how the Crown Jewels got into the Gallaghers' safe?" he asked, joining the girls at their table.

"Yep. He thinks that Patrick Gallagher stole the jewels in 1907, fled Ireland, and escaped to the States. His team is investigating it now, but he believes that the name Patrick Gallagher was an alias."

"That makes sense," nodded Derik. "Come here, hide the jewels here. But where did the letter come from, and how did Bishop get it?"

"Bishop's father was Patrick Gallagher's personal attorney. When Patrick died, his son Brian became the new owner of the jewels. Brian married and had two children, both of whom were scoundrels. According to what Connor Bishop told Detective Edwards, Brian Gallagher was so disgusted with his two sons that he created that riddle for them to solve."

"The handwritten clues!" exclaimed Derik.

"Yep. He told them that he had hidden a great treasure for them, and that upon his death, they would each be given a copy. Whoever could solve the clues would be the next successor to the Crown Jewels."

"So, how did Connor wind up with the clues and not the Gallagher kids?" asked Derik.

"Brian and his sons were killed in a plane crash. Connor Bishop's father, who had helped pen the clues, stole the paper with the riddle. A month later, he died of a heart attack, leaving the secret clues to Connor Bishop."

"What about Mrs. Gallagher? She wasn't involved in all of this, was she?"

"As far as Detective Edwards is concerned," said Ava, "she had no idea that the family had such a horrid secret."

"She's devastated, I'm sure," said Carol sadly. "An innocent victim."

"So, let me guess," offered Derik. "Connor tried to solve the riddle, couldn't do it, and came up with the idea of the contest to get help."

"You're exactly right," said Carol.

"Geez, a lot of good greed did them," said Derik shaking his head. "They were never able to sell the jewels, and they just kept them hidden in a safe."

"It's Kaitlyn," said Carol, grabbing her buzzing phone from the table.

Ava and Derik listened anxiously. They could hear the excitement in Kaitlyn's voice and then the sobs of joy.

"We love you," shouted Ava and Derik so she could hear them.

Carol ended the call and took in a deep breath. "London's surgery was successful." She grabbed her friend's hands. "I'm proud of us."

"I'm proud of us too," laughed Ava.

Carol's phone buzzed again. A long number appeared across the screen. "That's weird," she commented, staring at the strange number.

"Hello?" asked Carol tentatively into her phone.

"Hello? Have I reached Miss Carol Miller?" a man with a soft but cheerful accent asked.

"Yes," she replied cautiously.

"Is there a Miss Ava Clarke and a Mr. Derik Charter present as well?"

Carol hesitated, weighing whether to hang up or continue the call. "May I ask who is calling?" she asked flatly.

"Certainly. My apologies. Where are my manners? I am Dudley Walsh, the prime minister."

Carol hit the speaker button on her phone. "Mr. Prime Minister," she stammered, nearly dropping her phone. "Yes, we're all here. We're on speaker."

"Wonderful! On behalf of all of Ireland, I would like to thank you personally."

Carol looked at Derik, struggling for something brilliant to say, something worthy of the moment. Ava took care of destroying that moment.

"Your cereal is my favorite, your highness."

"Pardon?" asked the prime minister.

"Lucky Charms, your highness. Lucky Charms."

AUTHOR'S NOTE

The Crown Jewels of Ireland are real and were reported missing from the Dublin Castle on July 6, 1907. There are many fascinating stories and theories as to what happened to the jewels, and as of this writing, they have not been found. If you do happen upon them, you'll never need lunch money again. They're worth about a billion dollars.

If you get a chance to visit Lexington and Concord, Massachusetts, you can retrace the historical landmarks visited by Ava, Carol, and Derik.

The Lexington Minuteman statue is located in Lexington, Massachusetts, at the tip of the Lexington Battle Greens. The statue is indeed bronze and does feature a large basin that is now filled with beautiful flowers.

The Alcott House—or Orchard House—in Concord, Massachusetts is an amazing place to visit. Louisa May Alcott was such an incredible writer and inspiration to people throughout the world. The official website is https://louisamayalcott.org. Louisa Alcott did love owls, and there is indeed an owl painted (by her sister, May) on the mantel of her fireplace.

There are two Sleepy Hollow gravesites: one near Tarrytown, New York, and the other in Concord, Massachusetts. The story of the headless horseman and Ichabod Crane, written by Washington Irving, was based in Tarrytown, New York. In 1996,

North Tarrytown officially adopted the name Sleepy Hollow in honor of the story.

The Sleepy Hollow Graveyard described in this book is located in Concord and is a fascinating place to visit. You'll find the graves of numerous historical figures there, such as Louisa May Alcott and much of her family, Ralph Waldo Emerson, Nathaniel Hawthorne, and Henry David Thoreau.

If you visit the Ava and Carol Facebook page, you'll find pictures that I took at the Louisa May Alcott house, the Minuteman statue site in Lexington, and the Sleepy Hollow Cemetery. Ava and Carol's official Facebook page is facebook.com/avaandcarol.

We hope you enjoyed reading the sixth book in the Ava & Carol Detective Agency Series: The Crown Jewels Mystery. Be sure to check out our other exciting books in the action-packed series.

Previous books in the series

Book 1: The Mystery of the Pharaoh's Diamonds

Book 2: The Mystery of Solomon's Ring

Book 3: The Haunted Mansion

Book 4: Dognapped

Book 5: The Eye of God

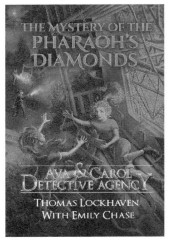 

If you enjoyed the book, please leave a review on Amazon, Goodreads, or Barnes & Noble. We'd love to hear from you! Thank you so much for reading our book, we are incredibly grateful!

Learn about new book releases by signing up at avaandcarol.com and following Thomas Lockhaven's author page on Amazon by clicking here.

Upcoming title

Book 7: The Curse of the Red Devil

Others by Thomas Lockhaven

Quest Chasers series

Book 1: The Deadly Cavern

Book 2: The Screaming Mummy

Printed in Great Britain
by Amazon

17365381R00073